PENGUI

THE BI

Robert Rodi is an advertising copywriter in Chicago, where he lives with a dog, two birds and a man. His other novels include *Fag Hag*, *Closet Case* and *What They Did to Princess Paragon*.

The
birdcage

A NOVEL
by Robert Rodi

BASED ON THE SCREENPLAY
by Elaine May

Ⓟ

A PLUME BOOK

PENGUIN BOOKS

Published by the Penguin Group
Penguin Books Ltd, 27 Wrights Lane, London W8 5TZ, England
Penguin Books USA Inc., 375 Hudson Street, New York, New York 10014, USA
Penguin Books Australia Ltd, Ringwood, Victoria, Australia
Penguin Books Canada Ltd, 10 Alcorn Avenue, Toronto, Ontario, Canada M4V 3B2
Penguin Books (NZ) Ltd, 182–190 Wairau Road, Auckland 10, New Zealand

Penguin Books Ltd, Registered Offices: Harmondsworth, Middlesex, England

First published in the USA in Plume 1996
Penguin Film and TV Tie-in edition published in Great Britain 1996
1 3 5 7 9 10 8 6 4 2

Printed in England by Clays Ltd, St Ives plc

Chapter
one

fortune's favor had descended upon South Beach again. After decades of neglect, the young and the rich, and those who loved the young and the rich, had returned, and brought back with them color and music and light and style. And those who had been there all along, those who had waited out the dry spell were ready—ready and waiting and dressed to celebrate anew.

Armand Goldman was one of those who had been here all along, and no one had been readier than he. He'd held on to his tiny property with both eyes fixed firmly on the future, and when the tide at long last turned, he flung open his doors and invited in the world. True, the years had deepened his tan into a kind of burnished leather armor and, while not thinning his hair, had somewhat silvered it; but he still cut a dashing figure (as witness tonight, in his loose black open-neck suit, looking something like a dandyish ninja); he was still fit to preside over the revels of those who worshiped beauty—whether God-given or, more often, conjured out of tubes and trunks and trickery.

All would have been, *should* have been perfect; but,

1

alas—Armand had a partner who had not weathered the wait quite as well.

He thought of that partner now, as he stood near the entrance of his minuscule nightclub, The Birdcage, and watched a sextet of his rather distinctive showgirls (The Birdcage's fabulously plumed "birds") as they writhed and cavorted while belting out a somewhat brotherly rendition of a Sister Sledge number.

Soon, it would be Starina's turn to perform. Brittle, impossible, unforgettable Starina.

It was Starina's face that had waited beside Armand all these years, waiting for the spotlight to return; an angular, aristocratic face it was then, with piercing eyes, a sharp, incisive nose, and a mouth ever open in ringing, raucous laughter. But the years had blunted the angles, thickened the flesh over the cheekbones, dulled the eyes, and flattened the nose. The mouth alone was unchanged. Armand looked for comfort, for continuity, to that mouth.

Yet despite the ravages of time, Starina still sought the ravishment of the crowd. When the time had come at last—when the curtains had parted and the music begun anew—the long-denied diva slapped on as much stage paint as possible, took the spotlight, and held it by sheer, naked need alone. A star in the manner of Garland and Piaf, Starina virtually fed off her audiences; and the spectacle was both so appalling and so endearing that audiences allowed it—even embraced it.

But *getting* Starina to the stage—that was the hard part. Death-row inmates walked the last mile with more good-natured pep.

"Good evening, Armand," said a silky, six-foot beauty as she passed into the club, on the arm of an admirer a good two heads shorter than she. Armand roused himself from his reverie, kissed her hand gallantly, and led her across the crowded club to a table abutting two

the birdcage

others. Smoke filled the air; Armand felt as though he were walking through water. It was a sensation he enjoyed—liquid, sensual, dark.

"Enjoy the show, my friends," he said as he helped the Amazon into her chair. What was her name again? Audrey? Andrea?

"We might like a bit to eat," she said, licking her top lip suggestively. "I find myself positively *ravenous.*"

He smiled. "Let me notify the kitchen—" Adrienne; that was it. "—*cher* Adrienne."

She beamed at him brilliantly, and as he moved away, he heard her mutter to her escort, "He knows absolutely *everybody.*"

Armand slipped through the mass of tables, blowing kisses and pressing flesh as he went, till he reached the kitchen door. Opening it and peeking in, he saw his hefty, middle-aged chef on his hands and knees, scooping a small chicken breast from the floor back onto a plate.

Armand scowled.

The chef noticed him, and shrugged. "If you don't want to know about these things, don't go spying."

"I don't not want to know about them. I want them to not happen."

"Get me a bigger kitchen. They won't happen."

"Lose some weight. The kitchen will be bigger."

The chef was about to respond to this when a waiter tapped Armand on the shoulder. Armand let the kitchen door fall shut, and turned. "What is it?"

"The Kennedys are here again for supper. It's the third time this week. Shall I give them a free round of drinks?"

Armand arched his eyebrows hopefully. "Ted?"

"No, just the younger Kennedys."

He sighed. "I wish we could get Ted." He nodded at

3

the waiter. "Give them a free round of coffee." Best to play it safe.

The waiter shuffled off, and Armand, now having completely forgotten the chef, made his way toward the stage. When he reached it, he pulled aside its black velour curtain and quietly stepped through; he was scarcely noticed, what with the full-throttle writhing of the six dancers.

The backstage area was narrow and cramped, little more than a corridor lined with cubicles and doors. The stage manager, Cyril, stood to one side, holding up a wig and costume, eyeing the stage. Armand approached him. "Where's Starina?" he asked.

Cyril turned and said, "Agador just called. She'll be down in five." Then he heard the final, ecstatic chords of the sextet's number, and recalled himself to his task. "Whoops?" he cried, as he leapt into action. One of the girls came flying offstage, tearing at her costume for a quick change. Under her discarded sequined bra was revealed a flat, shaven chest; under her flowing wig, a crew cut. And under her little silk skirt, a makeshift jockstrap of Ace bandages and tape.

As Cyril flung out the new wig and costume and stood by to collect the old, Armand dodged his way through the miniature tornado of textiles and peeked out at the audience. From this vantage point, he could see even more clearly that the club was filled to capacity. He'd have to start turning patrons away.

"You know," he mused aloud, "we should try for *three* shows on Saturday. Look at the crowd."

"Fine," said Cyril from the middle of quick-change melee. "But I get combat pay."

Suddenly, a door in the opposite wall flew open, missing the changing performer by mere inches: she was too obsessed with her wardrobe even to notice. A dark, barefoot young man in leopard-skin shorts stood at the bottom of the revealed staircase, panting heavily.

"Starina won't go on!" he cried. "She's still in her robe!"

Armand took a deep breath. "*Damn,*" he muttered.

"I don't know *what* happened this time," the young man said in real distress.

"Go back upstairs, Agador. Try to get her dressed. I'll be right behind you." He swung a little fist through the air. "Oh, *merde.*"

Agador hurried back up, his bare feet slapping against the stairs. Armand turned to Cyril and said, "Tell Carmen to get ready to do Starina's number, just in case. You understand?"

"Don't be stern," said Cyril, suddenly in some distress himself. "I'll fall apart. Oh, my God!"

Armand gave him a mollifying pat on the shoulder, then started up the stairs after Agador.

Yet again, yet again.

For someone who craved every moment on the stage as though it were her last, Starina's reluctance to actually make the trip from makeup lights to footlights was becoming an increasingly epic-sized paradox.

Maybe, thought Armand, it was all a bizarre kind of foreplay. Maybe Starina couldn't enjoy being onstage without first being wheedled, cajoled, and flat-out begged to go there. The way some women of Armand's generation could only enjoy sex if they've been wined, dined, and flattered into it.

Or so he'd heard, anyway.

He reached the top of the stairs, took a deep breath, and went forth to face Starina.

No.

He shook his head and forced himself to remember. Starina lived, *really* lived, only on the stage.

The real diva at the top of the stairs was Albert.

Chapter

two

—————

albert clutched his frilly, flimsy robe around him and darted away from Agador as though he were a man-eating leopard instead of a leopard-sporting man.

"Please," Agador begged him, holding out high heels and stockings, "just put these on."

"No, Agador," he said, his voice soaked through with melodrama. "Victoria Page will not dance the dance of the red shoes tonight. Or any other night."

Agador withdrew the shoes. "Just the stockings, then."

He dismissed them with a great, sweeping gesture. "Victoria Page is dead!"

Agador again halved his offering. "Just *this* stocking . . ."

"Do you know how she died?" He laughed softly. "Alone. Weeping for her lover. 'For each man kills the thing he loves . . .'" Suddenly concerned by Agador's stricken face, he said, "Have you eaten? You look haggard."

"*Please* . . ."

He grabbed a handful of packets from his dressing

table and handed these to the young man. "Here. These are supplements. I bought them for Armand, but . . ." His eyes filled with tears. ". . . that's all over now."

As if on cue, Armand called from the adjoining room. "Starina . . . *Albert!*"

Albert shrieked and lunged for the door to his room. Before Agador could stop him, he locked it and held his entire body against it. From the other side, Armand started knocking.

"Come on, Albert, open the door."

"Get out!" he cried, flinging his arms across the door to spread his weight more evenly.

"Albert! *Open* it!" The knocking grew fiercer.

Agador said, in the kind of tones he would have used on a small child holding a loaded revolver, "Let's open the door for him, shall we? Let's be nice."

"No! I don't want him to see me." He bit his lip. "I— I'm hideous."

Agador knew he should immediately tell him otherwise, but before he could summon up such gallantry, the door burst open, knocking Albert well into the room.

Armand stood in the doorframe, holding his shoulder like a soldier who'd been bayoneted.

Albert screamed wildly, then ran to the window and covered himself with a curtain.

"Do you want to ruin me?" Armand said sternly.

"Don't look at me! I'm hideous!" He kept adjusting the curtain to try to achieve the greatest coverage. "*Hideous.* Fat and hideous. Oh, Agador!" he said, turning for solace to the sympathetic houseboy. "I'm in such *pain . . .*"

"I know," said Agador kindly. "It will pass."

"It will never pass! I hate my life." He nodded at the packets Agador still held in his hands. "Don't forget to take those supplements."

the birdcage

Armand rubbed his shoulder and snarled at him. "Are you *crazy*? Do you realize there's a packed house down there?"

Suddenly he was Margaret Dumont, standing on his dignity. "That's all I am to you, isn't it? A meal ticket."

Armand let his eyes fall shut. "I can't *stand* this."

"Never mind about my feelings. Never mind about my suffering. It's just about 'your show.' Not even 'our' show. 'Your' show. Well, I want a palimony agreement, and I want it *now*."

Armand's eyes popped open in slight surprise; this was a new wrinkle in the ongoing trauma. "Well, I don't happen to have a palimony agreement on me right now," he said, trying not to sound too withering. "Would tomorrow be all right?"

"Don't use that tone with me!" He pulled the curtain up to his neck. "That sarcastic, contemptuous tone that means you know everything because you're a man, and I know nothing because I'm a woman."

Very carefully, so as not to seem vicious, Armand said, "You're not a woman."

"Oh!" Albert reeled as though struck in the face. "You bastard!"

Agador took pity on him. "Take it easy," he begged Armand.

Seeking an ally in Agador, Albert turned to him and said, "Whatever I am, he made me!" He pointed one painted fingernail at Armand. "I was adorable once. Young and full of hope! Now I'm this short, fat, insecure, middle-aged *thing*."

Armand stared at him incredulously. "*I* made you short?"

Cyril skidded into the doorway, panting for breath. "Okay," he said, "what do I do? The number's nearly over. Do I send Carmen on for Starina?"

"Yes," said Armand, sick of the whole ordeal.

Albert looked stunned by this betrayal. "No! How *dare* you?"

Armand gave Cyril a steely look. "Do it."

Cyril started back toward the stairs.

"No!" Albert shrieked.

Cyril stopped, and looked back with some confusion.

"Cyril!" Armand snapped at him, and he leapt into motion again.

"NO!" cried Albert, this time emerging from behind the curtain.

Cyril threw his hands in the air, and turned yet again.

Armand took a menacing step toward him. *"Now, Cyril!"*

Albert threw himself at Armand's feet. "Please! I'll go on. Don't give my number away. I'll be good. You'll see."

Armand took a deep breath, then made a mental note: *In future, call his bluff.* He turned to Cyril and, in a low voice, said, "All right. Put the mambo number on, and tell Dante and Beatrice to stand by with the staircase. Go."

Cyril, transparently relieved to have an uncontradicted command, flew toward the stairs as though he'd sprouted wings.

Albert held his hands before him. "Look, I'm shaking. Agador, I need some Pirin tablets. *Quickly.*"

As Agador raced to the makeup table, Armand threw Albert a disbelieving glance. *"What?* What are you taking?"

Agador unwrapped a Kleenex tissue to reveal two small white tablets. "Here," he said, handing one to Albert. "One before the show, and one after." Albert greedily took a pill and popped it into his mouth. "But," Agador added, folding up the remaining pill and slipping it into his leopard-shorts waistband, *"no more."*

He nodded gratefully, humbly. "Thank you, my darling Agador. Give me . . . a moment."

Albert picked up his high heels and stockings from the floor, and headed for the dressing table. Convinced that no further histrionics were coming, Armand and Agador turned quietly and started out. Armand took a piece of candy from his jacket pocket and stuffed it into his mouth as he went; the cool peppermint boosted his sense of relief.

When they were both in the adjoining living room, Armand shut the door behind them, then turned angrily on Agador.

"What are you doing? Why are you giving him drugs? What the hell are 'Pirin' tablets, anyway?"

Agador grinned conspiratorially. "They're aspirin! Aspirin, with the 'A' and the 'S' scraped off."

Armand considered this a moment, then opened his eyes wide with appreciative awe. "No!" he said. "My God! What a brilliant idea."

"Oh, it's the tip of the iceberg. You don't realize the miracles I perform with Miss Albert. I have him convinced that crushed mint leaves are a sleep enhancer. And that dried pomegranate seeds are a powerful Guatemalan hangover cure."

Armand regarded his houseboy with a newfound respect—at least, as much respect as he could muster for someone in leopard hot pants. "How do you manage it?" he asked.

Agador shrugged. "Simple. By not *telling* him that they're crushed mint leaves and dried pomegranate seeds. I make up exotic names for them. For instance, I call the mint leaves 'Opia Slumbra,' and I only let him have three pinches in hot water, because I say they're so potent that even a pinch more puts him at risk of never waking up again." He trilled a laugh, then held his hands over his mouth.

Armand shook his head in disbelief. "And that works?"

"Like a charm. I'm surprised he never mentioned it to you."

"Well, he knows how I feel about narcotics." Somehow, this sounded so ridiculously heavy-handed, in view of the fact that they were discussing mint leaves, that they both started giggling like schoolgirls.

Through the floor of the apartment, they could hear the mambo number reaching its first convulsive chorus. "Christ," said Armand anxiously. "What's taking him so long, anyway?" He went back to the bedroom door and flung it open.

Albert was seated at his dressing table, running a razor over his arms.

Armand thought his head might explode. He raced in and tried to snatch the razor away. "I don't believe this," he said. "You're shaving your arms *now?*"

Albert frowned at him and held the razor out of his way. "I didn't have time to wax." He resumed the operations. "Indifference is the most awful thing in the world, Armand." He took a final swipe up his forearm, then set down the razor and began applying mascara. "I've lost and gained over a hundred pounds in the last year," he continued, outlining his eye almost to his temple, "and I've yo-yo'ed from a sixteen to a ten to a sixteen again. And *you* never said a word through it all. Not one *hint* of encouragement or validation. If it wasn't for the Pirin tablets, I don't think I could go on." He set down his mascara brush and dropped his forehead onto his wrist, like an anguished Rodin sculpture.

"Albert," said Armand flatly, "I am going to kill myself if you don't finish making up."

the birdcage

"You don't love me anymore, Armand."

"Oh, Christ!" He turned and flung his hands at the ceiling.

Albert looked up, one eye enclosed in mascara, the other naked and buglike in comparison. "There's a man in your life, isn't there? I sense it. And I saw a bottle of white wine chilling in the refrigerator. I only drink red. And so do you."

Armand was growing really exasperated. "*There's no man!* I'm switching to white because red has tannins." He held out his watch and tapped it. "There are a hundred and fifty people out there, waiting for . . ."

Albert interrupted him by handing him an anklet from the dressing table with the exact measure of grandness Cleopatra would have used on a minion. Wordlessly, Armand knelt before him.

". . . waiting for you, ready to applaud you." Armand continued, as he tried to affix the anklet to Albert's foot. "To applaud the great Starina!"

Without warning, Albert kicked him, knocking him flat.

The breath knocked out of him, Armand lay on the floor for a while, recovering his wits; looming over him, he could see two Alberts—two Starinas—floating side by side for a few moments, before coalescing back into one.

"What do you do while I'm on the stage?" hissed Albert. *"Where do you go while I'm killing myself up there?"*

Armand began to struggle up. Albert, hearing his grunts, reacted as though he were a dangerous beast. "Go ahead!" he screamed. "Hit me! That's what you want to do, isn't it? Well, do it. Hit me! Go on! *Go on!*"

Armand, pushed beyond the limits of his endurance, let his arm flail wildly, without aiming. His hand connected flickeringly with Albert's shoulder.

Albert howled with terror and fell back, tumbling off

his stool and onto the ground, as if shot. Armand held his hand, wincing in pain.

"No more!" Albert sobbed, causing the one eye's worth of mascara to begin running. "No more! Please, no—no—" He broke off, perhaps sensing how ridiculously Tennessee Williams the scene had become, then looked with some concern at Armand. "Are—are you all right?"

Armand held out his hand. "I hurt my thumb."

Albert gasped. "Oh, my God, forgive me!"

"No, no," said Armand tenderly. "Forgive *me,* my little roundness, my little teddy bear." He crouched down beside Albert and took him in his arms.

"*Do* you love me?" Albert asked pathetically, resting his head against Armand's shoulder. "Swear that you love me."

"Of course I love you."

"Don't hurt me."

"No."

"My king."

"My queen."

The mambo number reached its second flourishing chorus, causing the floor to vibrate beneath them. The toiletries on the dressing table rattled in place. Armand kissed Albert gently on the forehead.

Chapter
three

He mambo number at last ended, in a whirling cyclone of furious ascending chords that resolved—or rather, dissolved—into a dizzying, dissonant scream. The audience, overwhelmed, applauded in exhausted pleasure.

Cyril stood in the wings biting his nails and checking his watch. Immediately behind him, two of the showgirls, Beatrice and Dante, stood poised on either side of a small, prop spiral staircase.

Cyril was about to instruct them to roll this staircase onto the now darkened stage, when he took one last glance behind him, and sighed.

He looked to the top of the staircase and said, "Climb down, Carmen. She made it."

He glanced back again, to see Armand and Albert silhouetted in the doorway.

Armand said, softly, "Go—go, my queen."

"My king," Albert cooed. And then Starina took over, like a demon possessing a host body, and wafted over to the spiral staircase.

Carmen, a statuesque and striking Africanness, had descended and was brushing off her leopard-print outfit—an outfit identical to the one in which Albert now appeared before her. Carmen gave short, squat little Albert the once-over, as if to say, *This* is what goes on instead of me.

"I am so sorry," Albert said, meaning it.

"You certainly are," said Carmen with a sneer. She turned on one heel and flounced away. Albert sighed his worthiest Joan Crawford sigh, and began his climb.

Cyril hit a switch, and the lights went out.

Armand stepped onto the stage, and stood before a free-standing microphone.

He allowed a moment for his eyes to adjust to the darkness, then looked out at the expectant crowd—at that sea of goodwill—and tried, quickly, to drink in their faces, their scents, the positions of their bodies; he'd waited so long for them, and now they were here, and like a long-lost lover returned from the sea, they were endlessly fascinating to him. At times like this, he almost understood the exquisite desire and terror that fought so hard for primacy in Starina's dizzy head.

"Ladies and gentlemen," he said, smiling like a proud father, "the one, the only, the incomparable—Starina!"

The applause that followed was like a cascade of water, hail on a tin roof, the clattering of a thousand hoofbeats on pavement. Armand, deliciously startled as always by its power, scooted off the stage; behind him, Beatrice and Dante (who were rather more muscular than their demeanor would lead one to believe) wheeled the staircase onto the stage.

As they did this, Cyril threw a new switch; a pinpoint spotlight revealed only the bottom step of the staircase. It then moved languorously up the stairs, one by one, higher and higher, until a pair of thigh-high leopard boots was revealed—then leopard gloves holding a leopard muff—and finally, the face of Starina, tremblingly, joyously alive, beneath a cunning leopard hat.

"Hello," said Starina in mellifluous tones. "I'm just back from safari." She waved the muff at her boots. "Like him? . . . Oh, don't look at me like that! *I* didn't kill him. He died. And left me everything."

The audience laughed appreciatively and Starina descended the ladder with studied grace. "Hello, darling," she said, peering into the audience. "Back again? How delightful! Oh, look at those teeth. You must be a Kennedy."

More laughter; at least one lusty hoot. Starina took the whole of the audience in her gaze now.

"Where are the adorable couple who are celebrating their anniversary here tonight?"

From a nearby table, a middle-aged couple raised their hands in giddy pleasure.

"Mon congrats, you sweeties," said Starina, fluttering her fingers their way. "*I* may be celebrating something myself, soon! I think I've found 'the one'—and he's *not* a white hunter, or the *gorgeous* pilot who flew me to meet the Sultan of Brunei, or even the Sultan of Brunei himself, who shall remain nameless." More laughter. "He's just a boy who works behind the counter of a Seven-Eleven near the airport."

She paused for one, coy moment, then lifted the microphone to her lips and began singing. *"I knew this grocery clerk, unprepossessing . . ."*

Armand stood in the wings, watching her—watching Albert. It was amazing; the fits and furies had gone now, as though they'd never been, and Starina was here, engaging in an almost primal exchange of energy with her audience. Audience?—acolytes, more like! For despite the rather ridiculous figure Starina cut in her leopard outfit, by the time she'd spoken five words to the crowd, they were hers, and she was their pagan goddess.

Armand nodded in approval; then, secure in the knowledge that Starina and her worshipers would be holding each other captive for some time to come, he backed toward the door to the upstairs apartment. He froze in place only once, when Starina seemed to turn and address one of the lines of the song to him. When she turned away again, he darted into the darkness and made it clear to the door, only to be stopped once more, when Carmen stepped into his path. It was evident that the girl was holding back angry tears.

"I just want to say," said Carmen, "very calmly, very quietly, that it isn't fair to make me get all ready to do Starina's number, and then take it away because Albert condescended to move his ass."

Armand felt a little spark of anger. "Don't you dare talk that way about Albert!" he said through gritted teeth. Then, immediately softening, he said, "And you're absolutely right."

He turned and bolted up the stairs.

Carmen stared after him, hands on her hips, a look of utter confusion on her face.

Chapter
four

It *was* a narrow escape, but a temporary one. Sooner or later, Armand would have to do something to satisfy Carmen—not to mention Lola, Kiko, Wilhelmina, and all the other girls who chafed under Starina's stardom. Certainly Starina was The Birdcage's chief draw, and her legend, while small, was legend nonetheless. Still, the other girls were building followings of their own, and Armand was feeling pressure not only from the girls themselves, but from his patrons, to give them more to do. Thus, the idea of that third Saturday show; but could he ever convince Albert to sit out a performance?

He shuddered at the thought of the row that would ensue; then he arrived at the top of the stairs, and shut himself gratefully in the apartment.

Agador was there, still in his leopard panties, but now wearing one of Albert's "big hair" red wigs; it loomed over his head like a crimson tombstone. He was out on the patio, holding a basket on his hips, taking down laundry from a clothesline and lip-synching happily to Starina's number.

Armand caught his attention as he crossed the apartment. "Get that laundry down," he said, "then go fetch the white wine out of the refrigerator and put it in a bucket with two glasses. And take the night off."

Agador jutted his laundry hip out even further, and scowled at him. "Why do you treat me like a servant?"

"Because you're my fucking houseboy."

"I prefer the term 'maid.' It recalls Jean Genet."

"Prefer what you want. You know what you are. Now hurry!"

Agador pursed his lips proudly. "My father was the shaman of his tribe, you know. My mother was a high priestess."

"Well, then, it was pretty dumb of them to move to New Jersey."

"It was, wasn't it?" He shifted the laundry to his opposite hip and continued plucking clothes from the line. "But they wanted me to have a career. When can I audition for you again?" He struck a theatrical pose.

"When you have talent," Armand said dismissively. He scanned the apartment, to make certain it was presentable. When his eyes came to rest on the patio again, he discovered Agador still standing there. "Will you *move,*" he said. "And take off Albert's wig or I'll tell him you're wearing it."

Agador narrowed his eyes and turned toward the staircase, then shot a baleful look back at Armand and said, "And *I'll* tell him you're seeing someone else while he's on stage, you *beast.*"

Armand considered answering this patent blackmail attempt, but knew that the only way to get rid of a queen was to give her the last word. And the important thing now was to get rid of Agador. *"Go!"* he barked.

Agador tossed his head proudly, then dropped the laundry basket where he stood, and made an excessively wiggly and irreverent exit.

Armand stood shaking his finger and called after him. "And don't lock the front door when you leave!"

Then he hurried into the bedroom, whipped off his jacket, sat down at the makeup table, and began frantically applying makeup.

From downstairs, he could hear Starina continue her patter. The words themselves weren't always audible, but Armand had heard these rhythms so many times, had heard laughter punctuate it in the same spots so often, that he knew beyond doubt exactly what she was saying.

". . . This next song is a hymn to love. In other words, a hymn to him." He could picture Starina on the stage, pointing to an attractive young man in the audience (the man in question doubtless blushing in embarrassment). "Or perhaps—him." She would now be pointing elsewhere, at another youthful dreamboat. The audience, as expected, tittered. "Or, my heavens, *him.*" Greater laughter. Then, "Let's just call it a hymn to them—by me, for you." A beat. "There may be a pop quiz on this later." More laughter. "Now, if any of you know the words, feel free to sing along." Here she'd put one foot up on a stool and rest her arm on her leg, Marlene Dietrich–style. "If you don't know the words, just look at my upper leg. I had the lyrics written there in case I forget; but my big old thigh has stretched them out so much, you should be able to read them, even in the back." More general hilarity; then an orchestral intro to some French song Armand never could remember the name of.

His makeup completed, he surveyed his face from several different angles. Not bad—not bad. Some of the worst of the crow's-feet eliminated. He looked almost forty again. In fact, if he held his head a certain way, with his nose slightly tilted to the two o'clock position on the mirror, he might almost be mistaken for thirty-five or thirty-six. Except for the silver in his hair. But some men in their thirties had silver hair, didn't they? There was no question of dyeing it at this late date, anyway; he was too well known. The gossips would eat him alive. And Albert!—Albert would tease him about it without reprieve until the crack of doom swallowed up the planet. Better to *shave* his hair than dye it.

He tilted his head downward again, and suddenly the decades fell back into place. He sighed, then got up, donned his jacket, took another panicked look at his watch, and, as Starina continued her French number downstairs, he hurried out of the bedroom. He checked to see that Agador had left the wine as instructed, then started fussing with the candles in the apartment, adjusting them so that the friendliest light would fall on his face.

So silly, to take all this trouble to impress Val—after all these years! As if it even mattered how he looked. As if—

"Hi."

Armand turned. There he was, in the doorway: Val. His heart swelled at the sight of him; the onrush of love fairly cracked him wide open. Armand rushed to embrace him.

They held each other for a brief moment, then Val gently pushed Armand away. He smiled, a smile full of impossibly white teeth, his skin an unblemished expanse of late-spring snow. And the eyes!—*angels* cavorted in his eyes.

"You keep getting better looking," Armand said, not wanting to embarrass the boy with too fulsome an appraisal.

Val shrugged. "Thanks. So do you."

"Oh, *no*," scoffed Armand. Then, he stood back and cinched his pants at his waist. "Really? I feel so bloated."

He glanced at his reflection in the glass door. "Do you really think I look good?"

Val, clearly accustomed to having to pile it on with a trowel, said, "Primo. Honest." He entered the apartment and made himself at home.

Armand beamed at him. "You're sweet." Turning his attention back to his beloved boy, he said, "I'm glad you let your hair grow." Then, a pang of responsibility: "Did you eat?"

"I'm fine." Val let himself sink into one of the flouncy sofa cushions.

"Would you like something to drink?"

"Beer, if you have it."

Armand bridled. "I do *not*. Talk about bloat! White wine?"

Val shrugged. "Swell."

Armand took the wine from the bucket. "Côtes du Rhone all right? I hope so—it's all I have." He laughed gaily, then stuck the corkscrew into the bottleneck.

As Armand wrestled with the cork, Val listened nervously to Starina's growling vocal, wafting up from the club below. "How long has Albert been on?" he asked with a trace of anxiety.

Armand pulled the cork from the bottle and smiled. "It's only his second number. And I gave Agador the night off. So we're all alone! As requested." He set the wine on the table before the sofa and moved the two glasses into place between them. "Since when do you like beer?"

Val leaned forward and clasped his hands. "Look, I have something to tell you."

Armand, poised to pour, now hesitated. "Yes?"

"And I don't want you to get—how you get."

Suddenly, he was seized by a feeling of great dread. He clutched his heart. "Oh, my God."

Val took a deep breath and said, "I'm getting married."

Time stood still.

"Hello?" Val said.

Armand, his eyes wide and fearful, said, "Yes . . ."

Val shrugged again, and said, "I didn't want to tell you over the phone." This brought no immediate response, so he took it upon himself to take the bottle from Armand and pour the wine. "It's a girl." Somehow, he felt that this should be clarified, though he couldn't say why. "I met her at school. A wonderful girl. A really great girl . . ." He took Armand's filled glass and handed it to him. "Are you upset?"

Armand drank the entire glass in three herculean chugs. "Yes," he said with a gasp. "But let me tell you why." He sat down across the table from Val and refilled his glass. "First of all, you're only twenty . . ."

Val shook his head. "Look, Pop, I know I'm young—but you've always said I was a very level-headed guy. And I am. I have job offers, I know what I want my future to be." He lowered his head and gave Armand a sly wink. "And I have an incredible role model."

"Oh, please." Armand could have slapped the boy for attempting such blatant manipulation. If only it didn't work so well!

"But I do! I'm the only guy in my fraternity who doesn't come from a broken home."

Despite himself, Armand felt a flush of pride rouge his cheeks, right through the pancake. "Stop flattering me. It's cheap." He turned away, afraid he might burst into tears. "Well," he continued; "this—this thing is a joke, isn't it? It must be. Yesterday you were this little fat thing in diapers, going down that slide with your 'quack-quack.' " He smiled sadly and turned back to Val. "Remember Mister Quack-Quack?"

Val nodded uncomfortably; clearly he'd hoped to keep things much less maudlin than this.

Armand put his hand on his chin. "I think Albert may still *have* Mister Quack-Quack somewhere . . . that box of things he kept of yours. Your report cards, all your drawings. Your first little Dior suit." He shook himself from his reverie and gazed on his son with pure *tristesse*. "And today you're getting married."

"Is it all right, Pop?"

Armand looked at him hopefully. "Does it matter?"

"Yes." This emphatically—with that intensity only the young possess. "I want to hear you say it's all right before Albert comes up and starts screaming."

Given an iota of power, Armand could not resist wielding it. "Well, I won't," he said with wounded pride. "I can't. It's too crazy. If you do this, you're on your own. Don't come to me, don't ask me for anything, I don't want anything to do with it." He crossed his arms and stared away from Val.

An awkward moment passed. Then Val slapped his thighs and said, "Okay. Well . . . " He got up, retrieved his jacket, and said, "Goodbye, Pop."

"Goodbye. Come here," Armand said, without even a heartbeat between the two sentiments. He leapt to his feet and engulfed Val in his arms. "You little fool! As if I'd let you go."

"Then—it's all—it's all right?" Val managed to muffle from somewhere within the embrace.

"Yes, yes, it's all right!" He released his son, lifted his glass high, and said, "Put down your jacket, and let's drink a toast to this catastrophe." Val regarded him with concern and he said, "I'm joking. It's all right, I swear." Val still didn't look convinced; Armand thought he'd better try a convincing show of interest. "What's the young lady's name?"

Val's face changed utterly. His smile broadened to the approximate size of a billboard, and his eyes lost all focus.

In a tone of voice that invoked more than informed, he said, *"Barbara . . ."*

Chapter
five

b arbara, are you crazy?"

It was a rhetorical question; for most of his life, Senator Kevin Keeley of Ohio had made a specialty of rhetorical questions. "Does my esteemed colleague really believe that welfare mothers are incapable of self-support?" and "Are we not a nation of bootstrap-pulling individualists?" and "Is military conscription really too high a price to pay for freedom?" had all tumbled comfortably from his lips, and all had called for, and gotten, applause instead of answers. Even now, as the indignant congressman addressed his very beautiful—his heartbreakingly beautiful—daughter, he expected that at some level she might . . . well, not applaud him, exactly, but recognize in his indignation some superiority of demeanor, some authority before which she must come to her senses and, simply, finally, submit.

"I repeat—are you crazy? It's out of the question. You can't get married! You're not even eighteen!"

The senator's wife wrung her hands; as expert as her husband was at posing rhetorical questions, so was she at wringing her hands. "Who is this boy, Barbie?" she asked. "When was the last time you saw him?"

"Please don't call me Barbie," Barbara said for what was surely the one-jillionth time. She hadn't really expected her parents to endorse her engagement joyfully, but their objections seemed even more pathological than usual. Each of them, in her eyes, had heard the news, then gone right off the deep end. Which is not to say that they hadn't had ten toes curled around the edge of the diving board for some years now.

She sighed, then tried to find a calm, peaceful place within herself, and to radiate that placidity outward, like a kind of psychic wave. "The last time I saw him was this afternoon," she said in even, self-assured tones. "At two o'clock. We've been sleeping together for a year." Why had she added that? A pinch of malice into the mix? Oh, well—it was out now. No use crying over spilled dirt.

"Good God!" said the senator, sitting down very hard. "Has he been tested?"

Mrs. Keeley clutched her throat. "Kevin!"

Barbara leapt into the fray. "Yes!" she said, forestalling any argument about the propriety of the question. "Yes, he's been tested. And so have I."

Mrs. Keeley screamed, and sat down herself. There was something odd about following a scream by sitting down; one usually followed a scream by leaping up. Mrs. Keeley was forever getting these things wrong. Both her husband and daughter looked at her in annoyance, then resumed their own confrontation.

"Look," the senator said, "this will just have to wait until after the election. I can't deal with this now." He waved a hand, like Pontius Pilate.

Barbara looked at him as though she hadn't understood a word.

Mrs. Keeley, apparently unchastened, inserted herself yet again. "Where does this young man come from, Barbie . . . ra?" She cleared her throat. "Who is his father?"

Barbara checked her cuticles. If she really was the adult she claimed to be, now was the time to come clean. Now was the time to look them straight in the eye and say, *His father is a Jewish homosexual named Armand Goldman who runs a transvestite club outside Miami.* But somehow, she knew that this would be a tactical error; best get them used to the idea in easy stages. Let this be stage one: Barbara is getting married. After they'd grown accustomed to that, stage two: her future father-in-law was of the tribe of Abraham. Stage three she didn't even want to think about yet.

She looked up at them—at their anxious, earnest faces—and said, "His father is . . . in the arts."

"Ah," said Mrs. Keeley, hopeful but awaiting further information. "The arts."

"Yes," said Barbara, amazed at how cool she was while telling a barefaced lie. "On the council." When they continued to regard her expectantly, she burbled out, "The Council of Cultural Arts."

"Really?" asked Mrs. Keeley, who was clearly too proud to ask for more information on any organization with such a confidently declarative name. Surely she ought to have heard of them already.

Her husband suffered no such insecurities. "Aren't they the ones who funded the Mapplethorpe exhibit?"

"No, no," said Barbara. "He's—um—a cultural attaché to Greece."

"*Really?*" said Mrs. Keeley, with more enthusiasm this time.

But the senator was less easily impressed with European connections. " 'Cultural attaché'?" he asked. "What the hell is that?"

His wife shushed him and turned to Barbara. "That—that's a diplomatic post, isn't it, dear? Almost like an ambassador? I wonder if we can get Melina Mercouri to come to the wedding. Isn't she still alive? What a shame all the Onassises—Onassisi?—what a shame *they're* all dead. How old is the little girl now? What's her name again? Something with an *A*."

"For God's sake," said the senator, "we do not want any 'Onassisi' at our daughter's wedding, especially if they're only twelve. Have some goddamned sense."

Mrs. Keeley flushed red, then asked Barbara, "What does the mother do?"

Barbara thought, *His mother is a middle-aged man who performs cabaret under the name Starina,* but when she opened her mouth what came out was, "She's a housewife."

Mrs. Keeley sat back and smiled. "Well, that's really refreshing, isn't it, Kevin?"

He scowled. "I don't want to *talk* about this now."

The telephone rang, interrupting them. Barbara, grateful beyond words for any excuse to halt the interrogation, snatched up the receiver. "Hello?" she said. Her father rose and hovered over her.

It was Val. "Have you told them?" he asked.

She wanted to say both yes and no, but it was more important to put Val's mind at rest than give him the whole truth right now. "Yes, I just told them," she said.

"Me, too," Val said. "My father's very excited. In fact, he's holding up his glass—his third of the evening, mind you—" Barbara heard someone laugh; Val's father? "—to toast us."

Senator Keeley, frustrated by his attempts to hear what was being said on the other line, had by this time crept over to a second phone in this cluttered family study. He pressed two buttons, and suddenly Val's voice came squeaking out of the panel speaker.

". . . I'll put him on," Val said. "Pop?"

As Val's father protested, "No, no, no," Senator Keeley said, "I thought his parents were in Greece."

Barbara, realizing what her father had done, covered the mouthpiece. "Dad!" she said, her lips curling in contempt. "Get off the phone!"

"Hello, Barbara?" It was Val's father. "Here's to your future!" Suddenly, the sound of breaking glass cascaded over the line. "Shit! I'm sorry. That wasn't my toast. I just broke my glass . . ."

Barbara adopted a cheerful, unperturbable tone for her parents' consumption. "That's all right! It was nice talking to you, and I'm sure we'll talk again real soon. Bye!" She hung up the phone and whirled on her father. "How dare you listen in on my conversation!"

The senator wasn't the least bit fazed. "You said his parents were in Greece," he said again.

She sputtered. "They are."

"You saw this boy at two in the afternoon, and now he's in Greece with his parents?" He gave her a Don't-con-me look.

She tried to quell her panic; he was on to her, and she knew it, and he knew that she knew it. "No," she said, pretending exasperation at his ignorance. "I—Greece? No. They're—they're *back* from Greece. For the winter. They're at their vacation house. In South Beach."

Mrs. Keeley looked hopeful. "Is that like Palm Beach?"

One more lie couldn't hurt at this point. "Close," said Barbara. "It's about two minutes from Fisher Island—where Jeb Bush lives."

Mrs. Keeley's eyes lit up. *"Really?"*

Barbara opened her mouth to respond, but she couldn't quite bring herself to affirm that "Really." These were, after all, her parents. Suddenly, she envied Val. With parents like his, clinging by their fingernails to the outer edge of society, all *he* had to do was convince them that his fiancée's family weren't ax-murderers.

Chapter

six

Armand sat on the patio alone, gazing at the stars and contemplating infinity. Or if not infinity, the endless cycle of life—of babies into men into fathers into—into—well, it didn't bear thinking on, not to any great extent. Not to someone who at some angles, in the right light, still looked forty. Or even thirty-six. But he found the sky comforting; it was beyond constant—it was unmovable. Someday, Val might stare at the same sky after his own son announced his engagement, and think, too, *It's just the way of the universe. We whirl, we spin, but up above—stillness.*

There certainly was little enough stillness below Armand; the floor began to shake with thunderous applause. He took a deep breath and slowly drew himself back to the present. Starina had no doubt finished her set for the night, and that could only mean that Albert would be bursting through the door at any moment.

Armand looked over his shoulder in expectation. It was then that he noticed the remains of the broken wineglass, still on the floor. He hadn't even had the good sense to clean up first. Well, he'd fetched himself a new glass, and that was really all that was important for now. He took a final swallow of the Côtes du Rhone, and put his chin on his hand.

Then he heard Albert's unmistakable clump, clump, clump on the stairs. Those ridiculous leopard boots. Armand had to suppress some giggles; he must be drunk indeed.

The door flung open, and the sweaty, limp, bedraggled remains of the great Starina spilled into the apartment.

Albert gazed about in a panic, then spotted Armand on the patio, espied the wineglass in his hand, and Val's wineglass on the table, right next to the empty bottle. Then he extended his leopard-swathed arm, pointed a daggerlike fingernail at Armand, and said, with a brilliant display of righteous indignation, "Ah-*hah*!"

Armand, knowing it would be useless, nevertheless said, "Wait . . ."

Albert picked up a ceramic vase and hurled it at Armand, who, knowing Albert's disgraceful aim, did not even try to duck. True to form, the vase crashed against the doorjamb, about three and a half feet wide of the mark.

Ignoring this embarrassing performance, Albert stamped his foot and shrieked, "Who *is* he?"

Armand winced and raised his hand. "Will you stop screaming! It's Val. *Val.*" Albert had apparently been enjoying playing his scene too much, because he looked at Armand now with not just suspicion, but a tinge of disappointment. Armand said, "He's in his room. Go on, check if you don't believe me."

Suddenly, Albert softened, and a smile tugged itself slyly across his face. Dear Val was here?

He turned and tiptoed to Val's room, the last door off the hallway, and crept inside.

Val was lying in the center of the bed, the covers pulled up to his chin; and if the boy's eyes were closed a bit too tightly to look quite normal, Albert didn't notice. He bit his lower lip and clutched at his breast, moved almost physically by the beauty of his dear baby boy; then he reached down and brushed some of the stray hairs from Val's forehead. Did Val flinch at this?—No, no; of course not. He was asleep.

Albert clasped his hands together and sighed happily; then he turned and saw the clothes strewn about the floor. He shook his head in loving exasperation, picked up each and every item, from flannel skirt to boxer briefs, and crept back out into the apartment proper.

"His hair is so *long*," he cooed when he was again within earshot of Armand.

"Yes," said Armand, who had now left the patio and was finishing off the wine in Val's glass.

"Why is he here?" he said, dumping the clothes in a hamper. "Did he say?"

"No," lied Armand. He put down the now-empty glass and immediately changed the subject. "How was the show?"

"Glorious. Oh, honestly, Armand," he pouted, "you really should have brought Val down to see!" He knelt on the floor, took Val's suitcase onto his lap, and opened it. "He hasn't seen my show in—God almighty, look at these dingy T-shirts! A good bleaching's in store for this lot."

Armand headed for the bedroom. "He wanted to surprise you, but he was too tired. And frankly, so am I. Good night, my queen."

"Good night," Albert said airily; he was now concentrating on sorting clothes. "Honestly," he muttered, "you'd think they had no laundry facilities whatsoever at that college of his."

Within minutes, Albert had a load of clothing ready for the washer, and was looking for the laundry basket. A quick search revealed that it was still on the patio, and that Agador hadn't yet finished taking down the shirts from the clothesline. Silly, dear Agador! Albert brought the basket inside, filled it with Val's clothes, then put as many as possible into the washer, poured in a good pint of bleach, and let the first load run through the cycles.

Then he returned to the patio and began carefully taking down the shirts Agador had left. But just as he was doing so, a sudden wind kicked up and blew one of the shirts—one of Armand's tuxedo shirts, mind you—onto the fire escape two floors down and to the right.

"Oh, poo!" said Albert. He looked at the shirt flapping contentedly on the railing and thought, It will never wait for Agador in the morning. So he climbed off the patio himself, descended the fire-escape stairs, and fetched it. Just as he did so, a car rounded the corner and caught Albert in its headlights; Albert put his hand up to fight off the glare, and thus missed the sight of the car careening into a lamppost, where its front end crumpled noisily.

"Filthy drunks. Shouldn't be on the road," he sneered as he climbed back up to the apartment, and it was only a few moments later, when the driver stumbled out of the car and began pointing at Albert and babbling to his dazed passenger, that Albert realized he was still in Starina's leopard outfit. Could he, in his heels and tail, scrambling about on an exterior staircase, have caused the accident by being too startling an apparition? Guiltily, he crept back inside and stripped off the leopard suit. He changed into his modest flannel nightshirt, then took another look in on Val, who was resting more comfortably now, thank God; one naked foot was hanging loose over the floor, and he appeared to be snoring lightly.

Too excited to sleep himself, he sat up for some time making a list of all the things he'd need to pick up the next morning to accommodate Val on this surprise visit. It did his heart good to have the whole family together again!

One shopping list, two loads of laundry, and three sneak peeks at Val later, he crawled into bed beside Armand, snuggled up against him, and slept more deeply and easily than he had in months; he didn't even need any Opia Slumbra!

Chapter
seven

The next morning Albert was up and active after no more than four hours of sleep; yet he felt unaccountably rested and energetic. He donned his favorite pair of mint-green slacks, a pristine white windbreaker, and a neckerchief, then got his canvas shopping bag and went marching down a narrow street lined with markets—the old markets, not yet displaced by the new, expensive ones favored by the tourists.

The shopkeeps—longtime acquaintances all—called out to him happily. "We've got some nice lobsters today, Albert!" "Fresh mangoes, just in this morning, Albert!" And at each one, he stopped and bought the best, the freshest, the finest.

"The chocolate truffles are still warm," said handsome old Heraclio. "Shall I put a pound aside?"

"*Two* pounds," said Albert proudly, his fingers in the air. "The piglet is home!"

At Alfredo's Grocery, Alfredo's son, Martin, smiled that brilliant smile of his and welcomed him in. "Hey, how you doin', Albert?"

"Fine, fine. How are you, Martin? Did the green tea work?"

"Perfect! Cleaned me right out. What can I do for you?"

"I want a nice, big roast. Val is home!"

Martin's eyes popped out in surprise. "The piglet! Well, then," he said, in a tone that indicated he would find an extra-special cut today, "let's see what we've got for a growing boy . . ."

The cut was fine indeed, well marbled and rich in hue, and must have been aromatic as well, for Albert was troubled by a very persistent mixed-breed who literally dogged his steps all the way to Mario's Bakery. "Mangy cur," he grumbled as he shut the mutt out on the street.

Inside, he picked out an enormous chocolate cake with butter-pecan icing.

"Would you like the cake delivered?" asked the dull-eyed clerk.

"Yes, please. And don't forget to write. 'To my Piglet, from his Auntie,' on it."

The clerk said, "You got it," but wrote nothing down; Albert narrowed his eyes in distrust. Where was Mario? Mario would have written it down.

But he chose not to make a scene today; he was too happy. He nodded and said, "Thank you. Well, I want to get back before he wakes up." Then, noticing a tray of free samples by the cash register, he said, "I'm just going to try this, then go." He took a pastry from the tray and slid it eagerly onto his tongue. Immediately he was assailed by the dark, indolent sensuality of truly fine chocolate. "Hmm!" he enthused. "Chocolate schnecken. A triumph. Well, bye bye!" The dull-eyed clerk stared at him so impassively that Albert decided to throw good manners to the wind. "Perhaps *one* more schnecken. Do you mind? . . ."

Meanwhile, Armand had finally dragged himself out of bed, struggled into a dressing gown that he could have sworn was fighting back, and staggered out of the bedroom, his head banging like a coffee tin with a golf ball in it. White wine and its damned sulfites! He shakily lit a cigarette and headed for the kitchen.

Agador was at the sink, wearing a colorful sarong. Armand plopped himself at the kitchen table and squinted disapprovingly at the sunlight. Agador brought him a cup of coffee.

He took a sip, his hand trembling only slightly. Then he twisted up his face like a croissant. "What is this? Sludge?"

"Yes," said Agador with sunny sarcasm. "I thought it would be a nice change from coffee." He leaned into Armand's personal space and purred, "You should have told me you were meeting Val last night, you *bad* man. I wouldn't have been so sassy."

Armand turned his head to reply and found himself staring at Agador's left nipple. "*Will* you put some clothes on!"

Agador waggled his bare chest at his employer. "Why won't you let me be in the show? Are you afraid of my Guatemalanness?"

Armand furrowed his brow and pushed the undrinkable coffee away. "Your *what*?"

"My Guatemalanness. My *heat*." He thrust his muscle-clotted pelvis at Armand. "Are you afraid I'll be too primitive for your little estrogen Rockettes?"

"Yes. Right," said Armand, changing his mind and taking the coffee back. "I'm afraid of your heat."

Agador pouted. "If you'd denied it, I'd have known you were lying."

Armand dared another sip. "And since I admitted it?"

He thought a minute. "It means you're lying, too, I guess. Oh, darn." He sulked away.

Armand sat for a moment, trying to sort through the boy's Byzantine system of logic. He hadn't got very far when Albert burst into the kitchen, carrying armloads of foodstuffs. "Yoo-hoo! Here I am! The bag lady!" he trilled happily. "Good morning, Agador!"

"Good morning, Madame," he said with a curtsy.

Albert rewarded this gallantry with a little kiss, then handed the bags to the houseboy. "Wash these, will you, dear? They're delivering the rest around noon. Good morning!" he said to Armand, giving him a kiss in turn. "My God, that beard!" He squinted and applied the soft back of his hand to his bruised upper lip.

He then went to the patio and peeked over the side. "Oh, shoo, you filthy flea circus!" he cried, flapping his hands. Then he turned and said, "A horrible dog followed me all the way home, sniffing the roast I got for Val. *Vile* thing. I could have been *savaged* . . ."

Armand wordlessly took another sip of sludge, and Albert proceeded to the dryer, where he took out the final load of Val's clothes and began folding them. Agador appeared with a cup of coffee, and handed it to him.

"Thank you, dear," he said, and, after a sip, "Hmm. Turkish. Delicious." He turned his attention to Armand as he folded. "Is Val still asleep? You should have told me he was coming! I'm so ashamed of the way I acted last night . . . but how could I know? The truth is," and here he paused in folding a pair of white boxer shorts to wag a finger at Armand, "you can't stand sharing your son with me. You're always pushing me away." He placed the underwear to one side and took an Oxford cloth shirt from the basket. "Oh, *look* at this shirt. It's a *rag*. No matter how many shirts I send that boy . . ." He tut-tutted and shook his head, then looked up and seemed to notice for the first time that Armand was slouched over the table, bags under his eyes. "You look awful. What's wrong?"

"Val's getting married." There. It was out.

Albert smiled, then giggled, then looked at Armand for clues that this was a joke. Finding none, he giggled again, more nervously, and said, "Don't be silly. I got a pork roast for dinner." He started folding again, this time more quickly, so that shirts got folded like underwear and vice versa. "I wanted to get filets mignons but they're so expensive. What do you mean, 'married'?"

"I mean—" Armand stopped, stumped, rubbed his forehead, then said, "What do you mean, what do I mean? I mean 'married.' "

Albert fidgeted, dropping the laundry to either side of him. "I don't understand."

"Yes, you do."

"*No!*" he screamed, his hands flying to his face.

Armand was ashamed to admit he was enjoying this—enjoying seeing Albert react more shamefully than he had. "Some girl he met at school," he said, just before taking another dip into the Turkish sludge.

"But he's a baby!" wailed Albert, tossing all the laundry he'd folded into the air. "He's too young! He'll ruin his life!"

Armand sighed. "We went through all that. The bottom line is, he's getting married no matter what we say, so the less said, the better."

Albert's eyes started darting around the room, settling on nothing. "Oh, my God. I woke up feeling so good and now—all of sudden, I feel . . . so *funny* . . ." He grabbed his chest and doubled over. "Ssh. Take it easy. Just breathe. *Breathe . . .*"

"I can have a team of paramedics here in three minutes," said Armand blandly. "The Academy Awards committee will take slightly longer."

Albert shot him a poisonous glance.

At that moment, Val entered, in tattered gym shorts, his hair an attractive jumble. He came out of a herculean yawn and looked at Armand, then at Albert. His face set to stone instantly.

"Oh," he said. "You've heard."

"Oh, Vallie! Oh, my God!" said Albert, leaping up and lunging for the boy, who backed up to avoid him. "This is such a shock. I'm not saying anything—I promised your father—but you're only twenty and if you throw yourself away on some dormitory slut, you'll be sorry for the rest of your life. There—enough said," he declared, forestalling any objections on Val's part. "No more. That's all. Subject closed. Well, don't just stand there! Give me a kiss! Or are you too grown-up for that now?"

Val waited a moment, to make sure Albert had got the hysteria out of his system; then, seeing only his smiling old Auntie, he said, "Hello, Albie," and gave him a kiss and a hug.

"Oh, Armand," said Albert, rocking the boy in his arms, "he's going to leave us. And we won't have any others."

Armand almost choked on a sip of coffee. "Not without a miracle," he quipped.

Chapter
eight

louella, the Keeleys' housemaid of over twenty years, brought the senator and his wife their usual breakfast of halved grapefruit and melba toast (her) and Captain Crunch with skim milk (him). But today, she had trouble getting their attention; they were, in defiance of three decades of tradition, actually watching television during mealtime.

"That be all?" she said to Mrs. Keeley, who turned, noted her presence, smiled wanly, and nodded, then turned quickly back to the TV screen.

"You're mighty goddamn welcome," muttered the housemaid as she padded out of the breakfast room.

The scene that had both Keeleys so riveted was of four men—two of them the program's hosts, one the senator himself, and the last the white-haired but by no means frail Senator Eli Jackson—on the set of a public affairs show. All four men were shouting incomprehensibly.

Finally, Senator Jackson made his voice, a booming, authoritative thing, heard above those of his interrogators. "When I—and Senator Keeley here—" The camera made a swift and perfunctory pan to alight briefly on the ramrod straight, crimson-faced Senator Keeley before swinging back to Senator Jackson. ''—when *we* founded the Coalition for Moral Order, it was to express moral rather than political—''

He was interrupted by both hosts nearly at once: one, a young, blow-dried baby boomer who said, ''Oh, come on; since when do moral views get campaign contributions?'' and the older, liver-spotted host who jumped on the younger by saying, ''Oh, *you* come on! Once the liberals abolished morality . . .''

Unable to contain herself, Mrs. Keeley whirled on her husband and said, ''It's a *wonderful* show.''

The senator waited until a lull in the dialogue to reply, ''The most intelligent show on television.''

Now he himself was on-screen, smiling at the camera as he had been taught, and, not relaxing his shoulders nearly enough, saying, ''I think what Senator Jackson is trying to say is that morality *is* political. Abortion, same-sex marriage, contempt for family values, pornography—they wouldn't exist if politicians didn't pass laws to protect them. And that's why both houses are now Republican . . .''

The two hosts began shouting at each other again. Senator Keeley, pleased with what had been the only sound bite he'd managed to squeeze in, now took the remote control and turned off the TV. He raised his eyebrows at his wife, as if to say, There it is, then picked up some papers and a tape recorder.

''*Bravo*,'' Mrs. Keeley said. She'd read in a magazine, long ago, that a wife must be her husband's biggest fan. ''It's a perfect platform.'' She tried to keep any desperation out of her voice.

''Yes,'' said the senator, sorting the papers. ''I'm very

glad I got on Jackson's bandwagon instead of Dole's. Dole is just too . . . too . . ."

Mrs. Keeley waited a moment, then daringly filled in, "Dark?"

Senator Keeley shrugged. "Actually, I was going to say liberal. But he's dark, too." Something in one of the papers caught his eye, and he jotted down a note. "I have to fire this woman . . ."

Mrs. Keeley shifted in her seat. "You know," she said nervously, "this boy that Barbie wants to marry . . ."

The senator ignored her and started speaking into a tape recorder. "Miss Porter, page two, second paragraph, is 'porno,' not 'pronto' . . ."

His wife, undaunted, barreled on. "I wonder if he's old money. I mean . . ." She cackled. ". . . a cultural attaché . . ."

A tap on the door interrupted them. They turned, and Louella reentered respectfully. "Your campaign manager is callin'," she said. "He says he's *got* to talk to you."

Senator Keeley nodded in understanding, and Louella left, once again without a thank-you.

Senator Keeley pushed back his chair, got up, left the breakfast table, and picked up the phone.

"Hello, Ben . . . Ready for what? . . . *What?*"

Mrs. Keeley stood up in alarm. "What's the matter, Kevin?"

He turned to her and mouthed the words *Jackson is dead*.

Once again, Mrs. Keeley screamed and sat down.

Senator Keeley turned away from her in irritation and put his hand over his exposed ear. "He died—in bed," he said, repeating what he was being told. "Whose bed? . . . A . . . a prostitute . . ."

"*No!*" Mrs. Keeley gasped.

Senator Keeley pressed his ear harder. ". . . And a

minor," he said, his voice becoming flatter by the second. ". . . and . . . black!"

Mrs. Keeley's voice dropped a full octave. "What?"

"A—prostitute," repeated Senator Keeley robotically. "Minor . . . black." He took a feathery breath, then hung up on what Mrs. Keeley could hear was a still-ranting voice on the other end of the line. He turned to his wife, stared at her for a moment as if he had never seen her before, then said, "I don't believe this. I don't *fucking* believe this. I'm ruined!"

Mrs. Keeley, remembering that magazine article, forced herself to shift from devastation to devotion. "Why?" she said, kindly. "You're not responsible. You can't be held responsible for Eli Jackson's private life."

Her husband shook his head in stunned disbelief. "Louise, I'm the vice president of the Coalition for Moral Order, and my cofounder has just died in bed with an underaged black whore." He paused a moment, to let the full horror of these facts sink in. "Just wait till the media get hold of this!" He turned his eyes to the heavens, as if in supplication, then dropped his gaze and said. "I could *really* use a piece of candy."

Chapter

nine

---

albert had a box of tissues ready, close by. The double-ply kind—so soft—and scented, too. Spring lilac. It wasn't like him to have prepared so well in advance. But these were especially trying times, and they required the redoubling of his every effort.

He sat, tissues at the ready, on the couch in the salon where Val and Armand had shared wine only eighteen hours earlier, and opened the scrapbook on his knees. He was confronted with a barrage of sweet, painful memories: Val as a baby, pink and plump, laughing; then as a young boy, shy and suspicious, hiding behind his inches-long bangs; then as an adolescent, newly fearless, newly gorgeous; posing with Armand and Albert; with other friends—with a *dog,* for God's sake . . .

Armand, seated at the piano, idly tinkling out some unrecognizable tune, said, "You're driving me crazy, Albert," and it was only when he heard this that Albert realized he was sobbing rather audibly.

He gathered all his strength and made a sacrifice to prove his strength: he took Mister Quack-Quack from his arms and placed him reverently on the glass tabletop.

But seeing Mister Quack-Quack there, all alone, so sadly alone, only increased Albert's already highly refined sense of loss. *"My baby,"* he burbled, and he wept, but this time quietly.

"Why don't you take a Pirin tablet or something?" said Armand, tired and a little hung over. From the kitchen came the sudden, tinny noise of a television news show. Armand stopped tickling the ivories long enough to shout, *"Agador! Turn that thing off!"*

But Agador, in the kitchen, merely swiveled toward the door to the living room and stuck his tongue out, then turned back to the fascinating story on the tube, where a young black girl was now facing a swarm of overeager reporters.

"He looked kinda funny," said the black girl, her lips twisted up in partial amusement, partial TV coyness; "but he was smilin', so I didn't worry . . ."

The picture froze on the girl's crooked smile, and a voice-over brayed. "Senator Jackson's last words—tonight, on *Inside Edition!*"

Back in Dayton, an exhausted Louise Keeley said, almost in admiration, "How do they get them on so *quickly*?"

Her husband, who for the first time in living memory had not only loosened his tie but undone his first two buttons, said thickly through a mouthful of chocolate kisses, "They pay."

Louella stepped into the room and said, "Dinner."

Neither the senator nor Mrs. Keeley so much as looked her way.

Knowing that the day the senator grew indifferent to food was the day the world would crack in half, Louella trotted back to the kitchen to prepare herself for the ultimate emergency.

The report clipped along, and Mrs. Keeley, remembering what the magazine had said about putting things in a good light, said, "They're not mentioning you much."

Keeley shoved another handful of kisses into his mouth. "It's early."

Chapter
ten

───────

armand was at a crucial point in measuring out ingredients for his recipe, when a shriek from Albert almost caused him to spill vanilla ruinously:

"Oh, no! They wrote 'Uncle'!"

Armand turned in annoyance and alarm, and saw Albert standing horror-stricken over the cake that had just been delivered. He pointed to the newly opened cakebox.

"I told that little dope fiend 'Auntie,' Armand! And I get 'Uncle'!" He rolled his eyes and his fingers fluttered into the air! "*Uncle!* Val won't know who 'Uncle' is!"

Armand sighed, then turned back to his mixing bowl and carefully resumed his mixing. "He'll probably eat half the cake before he looks at it," he said. "He's just like you."

Albert smiled, flattered. "Yes, the piglet," he said. Then his face fell into a sudden frown. "We'll have to *completely* redecorate his room, you know. We can't put a married couple in a room that looks like a bulletin board." He shut the cakebox and shoved it aside. "Plus, there has to be room for the grandchildren! So there goes your den."

Armand rinsed his hands under the faucet and grinned. "Someone's feeling better."

"Well, grandchildren," said Albert dismissively. "They have that effect on one. I've even been busy thinking up names. If it's a boy, Montgomery or Antonio. If it's a girl, Eartha or Liza."

"Albert, they not only aren't pregnant yet, they aren't *married* yet." He doffed his apron.

"Oh, you! Where's your sentiment? You have to get into the spirit of things!"

Armand pinched him. "I'm in the spirit of things."

"Ho ho. I can just see you as a grandfather: pushing the carriage, gold chains clinking, chest hair dyed . . ."

Armand leaned against the counter and looked suddenly wistful. "Not a bad sight, is it?" Albert reached over to the mixing bowl and lifted the spoon. "Don't stir that."

"I wasn't going to stir it, I was going to taste it."

"Leave it be. It's the marinade. Go get ready for the rehearsal." When Albert showed signs of resisting, he deepened his voice. "Go on."

Albert dropped the spoon and narrowed his eyes. "You never let me help you cook." He wiped his hands on his trousers and stormed toward the door.

Armand laughed at his back. "Go, go, go. I'll meet you downstairs—Grandma."

When Albert had gone, Agador came waltzing in wearing a Heidi-style peasant dress with no blouse. "Hello, *mein herr,*" he said to Armand with a curtsy.

"I don't know where you find those things in your size," said Armand.

"You tease me, *mein herr.*" Agador went to the cupboard and got out his apron. "What's there for me to do?—Oh, I see someone has been cooking. Safe for me to enter the kitchen and clean up, is it? No toxic fumes?"

"Ha ha ha," said Armand without mirth. "I'd like to see you do as well."

"Oh, I'm a whiz in the kitchen. As good as in the bedroom." He turned on the water and started it running hot, then squeezed in a dollop of dishwashing liquid. "I've been thinking of names," he said excitedly.

Armand rolled down his sleeves and prepared to go. "Have you," he said. "Names for what?"

"The *child,* fool." He wiggled his butt at Armand but kept his hands in the sink, working. "If it's a boy, Leonard or Babatundi. If it's a girl, Hatshepsut or Lysistrata. Or Darlene."

Armand scowled at him. "You'd better learn to stop eavesdropping."

Agador wrinkled his nose at him. "Go on. You like me naughty."

Fed up, Armand left him to his chores, and went to take a nap.

Chapter
eleven

Well, it was exciting—Louise Keeley had to admit that.

Before he left, her husband had told her that she must on no condition look out a window. *Any* window. She had chafed under this prohibition for exactly four minutes and twelve seconds before sneaking a peek out the tiny window in the guest bathroom. The split second she did so, a dozen shutters sounded, capturing her image for the next day's front page. Feeling that a tiny bathroom-window head shot was undignified, she felt obliged to defy Kevin's orders once again, and show herself in her best Escada dress at the dining room window, a copy of Emily Dickinson in hand, and an apple. As the cameras clicked, she thought, There! That's better.

The small army of TV and print reporters, cameramen, and television trucks had been encamped on the grounds of the house for the better part of the day. Mrs. Keeley had been virtually trapped here, and was beginning to worry about her husband. It was exciting, all this activity, but it was also awful; she had to keep reminding herself how awful it was.

She'd just combed out her hair and was considering another accidental stroll by her bedroom window, when Barbara knocked and, without waiting for an invitation (college manners!), entered. "Where's Dad?" she asked.

"He snuck out this morning to meet with his advisers," she replied a bit testily. "They refused to come here."

Barbara tugged her bare foot across the carpet, leaving a little reverse-grain slash on the nap. "Mom . . . ?" she said, a bit plaintively.

"I should never have let him go," Mrs. Keeley said, wringing her hands. "How will he get back in? And me— I'm losing my mind in here, with nothing to do but wait and wonder!"

She sat down on the bed, and Barbara sat next to her. "Mom," the girl said in a small, anxious voice, "I have to tell you something . . . about Val's parents." It was time for stage two of her time-released revelations, she'd decided: time to play the Jewish card.

But her mother seemed not to hear her. "They can't blame us for this," she said, staring into space. "Eli Jackson was a common redneck, and we had nothing to do with him, socially." She looked hopefully at the window and said, "They understand that, don't they?"

Barbara nodded. "I'm sure they do."

"Thank God they're not snobs," said Mrs. Keeley.

"No," said Barbara, seizing the moment; "a snob is a terrible thing to be, isn't it? And while we're on the subject, there's something I need to let you know about Va—"

She was interrupted by a tap against the room's back window—the one facing the orchard.

They turned their heads and took in the rather alarming sight of Senator Kevin Keeley knocking at the pane while hanging on to a branch of a tree. His face was dirty and his jacket crushed.

His wife and daughter leapt from the bed, raced to the window, and opened it. He immediately hooked his arms over the sill and let out a sigh of relief.

"What are you doing here?" asked Mrs. Keeley.

The senator, with perhaps a touch of pride at his cleverness and daring now that he was out of danger, said, "I came through the orchard and over the top of the barn."

His wife clasped her hands over her mouth, then removed them and said, "But it's so dangerous! You could have fallen!"

He shrugged manfully. "I did."

Concerned lest there should be another such mishap, his wife and daughter now pulled him indoors. Mrs. Keeley hoped no photographers were below to catch anything so indecorous as her hand desperately yanking on her husband's meaty left buttock.

Just as they were hauling his final leg in, he cried out from his dangling position beneath the sill, "Don't let the ladder drop! We may need it." They didn't let the ladder drop, but they did drop the senator. He landed on his head and yelped in pain.

They helped him up, and once he gained his footing, they all stood panting together for a moment. Finally, he shook his arms and said, "I'm just a wreck! This is all anyone can talk about."

"Kevin," said his wife, "if we can manage it—there may be a solution."

He half-laughed at her as he doffed his jacket. "What? Death? Didn't work for Jackson."

She caught the jacket as it dropped from his back and said, "What about a wedding? A big, white wedding!"

He turned and gave her a bewildered look. "What

do you mean? What wedding? Who's getting married?"
Barbara cleared her throat and gazed at him adoringly,
and he said, "Oh, no. No!"

"Why not?" whined Mrs. Keeley. "It will restore your
image! A wedding is—is *hope.*" She smiled brilliantly. "A
white wedding is morality, and family, and tradition.
And—this would be such a special marriage, Kevin. The
son of a cultural attaché—a kind of diplomat, actually—
who doesn't look down on us because of Senator Jackson, who's willing to join our family. There's the cover of
People and *Time* and *Newsweek*—right there!" She
paused to allow this to sink in. The senator had sat himself on the bed and unlaced his shoes, and now was
staring at the floor in what appeared to be solid consideration of what she said; so she continued. "Love and opti-
mism versus cynicism and sex. It will be an affirmation.
If necessary, we'll get the pope's blessing. It's not too
hard."

"I know," said the senator weakly. He'd obviously
accepted the idea. "But the pope's too controversial. Billy
Graham . . . ? No, too liberal."

"Now, wait a minute," said Barbara, whose idea of
acceptance stopped shy of them planning the wedding
for her.

"Listen, Barbara," her mother said with sudden seriousness, "you have three and a half years till you're
twenty-one, and you want to get married now. Well, all
right. But there's a condition: let us do the thinking for
you."

"Where's the candy?" asked the senator.

"You've had enough candy," Mrs. Keeley said deci-
sively. Both her husband and daughter now regarded her
with curiosity and a smidgen of fear. She seemed to have
left her silly and indecisive side behind her now that
she'd gotten her husband's approval to plan a big society

wedding. She turned to Barbara now and said, "This boy, what's his father's name?"

"Armand," Barbara began. Then she swallowed and reminded herself, *stage two, stage two,* but what came out of her mouth was not Goldman. "Coleman," she said, wishing she would die. "Armand Coleman."

"Really?" her mother said, delighted. "I wonder if they're related to Bobo and Tish Coleman. Are they from Boston?"

"I don't think so."

Mrs. Keeley, now in command, said with newfound authority, "I think we should go down to South Beach and meet them, immediately. We can have dinner with them and spend the night with the Bushes." Her eyes glowed with anticipation. "Mr. and Mrs. Armand Coleman of Greece and South Beach!"

Chapter
twelve

$\mathbf{t}$he great Starina had got through nearly the entire number without a fit of prima-donna egoism, so that Armand, watching the rehearsal from a nearby table, thought that maybe, just maybe this was a break-through—a precedent, even. He should have known better.

The dancer was apparently the problem. As Albert, in his beaded gown with the feathered ruff, lounged on Cyril's piano and declaimed the lyrics to Armand's new song, the dancer—one "Celsius"—whirled about in his tights and sleeveless T, showing off his hard, lanky physique as though he were offering it to the highest bidder. He wasn't merely upstaging Albert; he was outdazzling him, as well. Albert might be drenched in glitter and down, but Celsius—Celsius had abs.

When the dancer executed one bump-and-grind too many, then turned over his shoulder and actually *winked*, Albert broke off singing. He slipped off the piano and stormed to the front of the stage, leaving a confused Cyril to trickle to a stop.

"Well, this is impossible," he said, huffing and gathering up his voluminous sleeves. "Either I'm an artist or I'm just some cheap drag queen playing it straight so *he*"—and here he made a catlike swipe in Celsius's direction—"can get some laughs."

Armand took a stab at diplomacy, knowing it was useless. "Let's just try and get through it . . ."

Albert winced, then placed two fingers on his forehead and stifled a moan. "You always ask so much of me, I have to understand every nuance of a song, I have to rehearse in full costume. But everyone else can just 'get through it.' I mean—he's chewing *gum.*"

Celsius flashed a roguish grin. "Chewing gum helps me think," he said, tossing in a few chomps for good measure.

Albert looked disdainfully over his shoulder at him. "Sweetie, you're wasting your gum."

"All right," said Armand, stepping in to prevent a catfight, "let's just take it from the top, no more talk . . . from *anyone.*"

Albert took a deep, menacing breath, then nodded to Cyril, and they began the song anew. Celsius danced with more circumspection this time, but Armand would have to keep an eye on him.

Someone tapped Armand on the shoulder. As he turned, he thought. What now?

It was Val. "Pop, I have to talk to you."

Wonderful timing. "Shh," he said, his voice low. "Sit down."

"It's important," insisted Val.

"Wait! Can't you see Albert's rehearsing?"

But it was too late for Val to disrupt the chanteuse; he was already disrupted. "Armand, did you see what he did?" he shrieked, peering over at the table. "Oh," he said, softening, "hello, Vallie darling."

"Hello, Auntie. You sound magnificent."

"Let's keep going," Armand said desperately. "What did Celsius do?"

"He blew a bubble with his gum. While I was singing! He can't *do* that while I'm singing." The inevitable tears began to flow.

Armand reluctantly pushed back his chair, got to his feet, and faced down the dancer. "Celsius, look . . . this may be a drag show, but it still has to be a good drag show—if possible, a *great* drag show . . ."

"Yes!" snarled Albert. "And just because you're eighteen and hung doesn't mean you're qualified to—"

"Let me do this, Albert," said Armand, interrupting him. "Celsius, this is a complex number. Full of mythic themes." The dancer seemed to swallow a guffaw; Armand decided to ignore this. "You were *invented* by the woman who's singing, you're her fantasy, this gorgeous fantasy, free and arrogant . . . and then suddenly, you, the fantasy, see her, your inventor; and she becomes *your* fantasy."

Celsius regarded Armand with some amazement, then turned and looked at Albert for what seemed a tad too long an interval. Then he turned back to Armand and said, "I don't think I get it."

"Try more gum," muttered Albert.

"That's enough!" barked Armand. He turned back to Celsius. "Well, you have to explore it, son. But start with the premise that, when you see this stunning, smoldering creature"—he gestured toward Albert, who adopted a dramatic pose to aid the demonstration—"she transcends your desire to chew. She electrifies you; something begins in your pelvis that travels straight to your heart." He took a breath, then added, practically, "But hit the pelvis."

Celsius nodded, nodded, nodded till Armand had

the birdcage

finished, then said, "But what do I *do*? I don't want to just *stand* here like—an object."

Armand bit his lip and tried not to show his frustration. Then he smiled and said, "Do this!" He went through a series of dance moves with what Val, distracted though he was, couldn't help but think was uncanny grace; he never knew his father was so light on his feet. "Five, six, seven, eight," said Armand, spinning, dipping, twirling, and bowing. "And this!" He leapt up to the stage platform. "A little Martha Graham, a little Fosse, a little Madonna—a stunning, eclectic celebration of dance." He made a series of aggressive, masculine circles, ending up before Albert, to whom he said, "And you, of course, sing." Then he circled away, and looked as though he might continue through the entire routine.

Val couldn't wait for that. He said, *"Pop,"* with a note of real urgency.

Armand stopped, dropped his arms in what may have been exhaustion but was probably exasperation, and said, "Coming." He turned back to Albert and Celsius for one last command. "All right. Try it again. I'll be right back."

He straightened his lapels and went to join his son, who took him by the arm and led him up the stairs.

"Well?" asked Armand, as they climbed.

"Barbara is coming with her parents," said Val, his voice trembling.

He stopped. "When?"

"They'll be here tomorrow."

Armand shrugged. "Well, that's plenty of time. Is that what you interrupted me for?"

"No," said Val, shaking his head insistently. "There's more. Please, keep going."

Armand grimaced, then resumed climbing.

When they reached the apartment, Val entered and

61

went straight for the bar. "Wine?" he asked, taking a partially consumed bottle of Sancerre from the bar.

Armand, keeping his ear cocked for any hint of a disturbance downstairs, said, "No. Hurry. Let's hear it."

"I think I'll have some." He pulled the cork and filled his glass.

Armand tapped his foot loudly.

Val took an emboldening swig, then made a face and said, "I wish you'd get beer." He wiped his mouth with the back of his hand and said, in one big gush, "Barbara's father is a conservative senator running for reelection and she told him that you're a cultural attaché to Greece and Albert is a housewife." He took another gulp, finishing the wine.

Armand reeled. "What?"

"She had to, Pop," he said pleadingly. "He's a founder of the Coalition for Moral Order."

"I don't care who he is. I don't want to be someone else. That is what you're asking, right? You want me to be someone else?"

Val's face burned with shame. "No, of course not," he said unconvincingly. He refilled his glass and sat down. "And neither does Barbara. But her father . . . Pop, her father is *Kevin Keeley*."

Armand didn't bat an eye. "Who's Kevin Keeley?"

Val groaned. "Do you *ever* read the newspapers?"

"Of course," he said, a bit defensively. "*Variety,* the *Star,* the Arts and Leisure section of the *New York Times* . . . Why? Is there something I don't know? You're not marrying some Nazi, are you?"

"No, no," said Val with a nervous laugh that did nothing to reassure him. "He's just . . . a conservative. Like half of America. And I'm not marrying him, I'm marrying Barbara." He looked up at his father sheepishly. "And I need your help."

Armand shook his head and took a step toward the stairs. "Not for this."

Val stood up. "You've done it before!"

Armand looked at him, astonished. "What? Lied about who I am? Never!" He bridled, and tugged at his sleeves.

Val grinned at him. "Oh, no? Remember my first day at Edison Park? What you told me?"

Armand, sensing that he might have entrapped himself, said, "No."

"You said that if Miss Donovan asked me what you do for a living, I should say you're a businessman."

Oh, that, thought Armand, remembering. "Yes, I did," he said guiltily. "Because you were a baby and Miss Donovan was a small-minded idiot, and I didn't want you to get hurt. That doesn't mean I was proud of lying. And anyway, it's different now. You're a man."

Val gave him his most soulful look. "But I can still get hurt."

Armand found himself incapable of reply.

"Pop," Val continued, in friendly, let's-stop-fighting tones, "it would mean everything to me if you'd just help us. Just for one night."

Armand felt the walls closing in on him; it was so tempting to give in to this boy, this beautiful boy so close to his heart. But he had his pride, damn it, and his dignity. He mustered his courage and said, "This is insane! What am I supposed to do? Close the club and pretend I'm a cultural attaché? Whatever the hell that is? Make Albert into a *housewife*?" He nodded vigorously at this last point, as though it were the peak over which no one could climb.

Val was relentless. "You have to send Albert away for a few days," he said in a low voice. "We'll *never* get him past the Keeleys."

the birdcage

This was really the end. Val might be his son, but he had crossed the line. He shut the door to the stairs, as though Albert might hear this treachery. Then he said, "Are you crazy? Albert?" He shook his head. "You *try* sending Albert away."

Val was well into his plot now, though. He looked around the apartment. "And you'll have to get rid of a few things around here . . ."

Everything the boy uttered was a new offense. "*What* things?"

Val pointed to the gold phallus on Armand's chain. "Well, that, for example." Then he walked across the dining room to a replica of a nude Greek kouros. "And this—"

"The Greek? But—that's art!" He shook his head. "And besides, if I'm a cultural attaché to Greece, it's not out of line to have Greek art."

"Well, what about the Tom of Finland print in the bathroom? Or this thing here?" He pointed to a primitive Middle Eastern sculpture with a large, erect penis.

Armand reached out, gripped the penis, and gently rotated the sculpture so that it faced the wall. "There," he said. "That better?"

Val sighed. "No. Look—it's not just one or two things. It's everything. I mean, you'd have to tone it all down, make it more like . . . *other* people's homes . . ."

"So we need a total redecoration now? To make us more like *other* people?" Armand could hear his voice ascending to a kind of high-pitched wail.

Val shrugged in apology. "And you have to—you know, to be a little less . . . obvious."

"*Obvious?*"

"Yes. Change your mannerisms a little."

The tension in the apartment was like the static between two just-washed socks. "What do you mean? I'm *obvious*?"

"Pop . . ." Val tried to think of a way to explain, then decided a demonstration would be more effective. He came up to Armand, ran his fingers down his cheek, then smeared the makeup from his fingertips onto the wall behind him.

Armand gasped at the sight. "Val, I just had the walls sponge-painted!"

There was a knock at the door; in this atmosphere, it sounded like the report of a rifle.

"Yes!" Armand snapped.

Cyril stuck his head in. "You better get downstairs. She's trying to take his chewing gum away."

Armand wanted to rip his hair out; he was assailed from all sides. He said, "I'll be right there!" Then, when Cyril had gone back down, he turned to Val and said, "Yes, I use foundation. Yes, I live with a man. Yes, I'm a middle-aged fag. But I know who I am."

"Pop," Val started to protest.

Armand stopped him. "It's taken me twenty years to get here, Val, and I'm not going to let some idiot senator destroy it. Fuck the senator! I don't give a damn what he thinks!" His eyes narrowed. "I know that kind. Their intolerance always catches up to them. Lays them flat. Sooner or later. You mark my words: sooner or later he'll get what's coming to him."

Chapter
thirteen

arry Radman had one great advantage, as a journalist: despite his large frame and inelegant gait, he could make himself virtually inconspicuous. It had served him well in the past, and it served him well now, as, trench coat flapping, munching on a sandwich, he wove his way between the camera trucks and news crews that were parked outside the iron gate of the Keeley house. He would occasionally pause and listen to what a newscaster was saying on the air. He wasn't chased away; no one asked him what he was doing there. He blended in; he observed; then he melted away.

And as he did so, a surge of excited confidence came over him. Here was an ice-cool blonde, very stern, intoning into her microphone, ". . . still outside the home of Senator Kevin Keeley, cofounder of the Coalition for Moral Order, waiting for the return of . . ."

Here, a suntanned, chisel-faced eight-by-ten glossy type, utterly serious and utterly fatuous at the same time, declaring, ". . . as yet no appearance by Senator Jackson's close friend and colleague, Senator Kevin Keeley . . ."

Here, a battleship-gray ex-anchor sort, trying to

sound congenial and in-the-know: ". . . no sign of Keeley, although an earlier report placed him at the home of Senator Robert Dole this morning."

Radman almost did a little skip over to his chosen vantage point. All of these officious, self-important fops, waiting for An Appearance By or Some Word From, as though they were helpless to get off their gym-trained duffs and discover what's what for themselves. That, of course, was Harry Radman's specialty.

And he was about to prove it. He tossed the remainder of his sandwich (just the crust) onto the manicured lawn and resumed his place against a maple tree at the far edge of the property. From here, he could see a liveried chauffeur carrying a suitcase and heading for the garage. He looked around. As he expected, none of the others could see the garage, or what was going on there. The Keeleys had turned on the floodlights in front of the house, and everyone had clustered there, like mindless moths. Harry, though—Harry knew a red herring when he saw one.

He gathered his trench coat around him, becoming inconspicuous again, then stole up to the gate and stuck his hand through the grillwork, waving a wad of cash back and forth. Within a few seconds, the chauffeur, who was packing suitcases into the trunk of the car, turned and spotted him, spotted the bills, and had a two- or three-second moral dilemma; Harry could pratically see the wheels turning in the man's head. But in the end, of course, the chauffeur looked over his shoulder, stood up straight, and came out to meet Harry.

Harry withdrew the bills to the point at which he could snatch them away, if necessary. "Where are you driving him?" he asked the chauffeur.

The chauffeur eyed the money hungrily. All twenties;

at least six or seven. "South Beach, Florida," he said. "Tonight."

Radman almost gingerly handed the bills over. The chauffeur took them, nodded, then returned to his duties in the garage.

Radman returned to his car by the same route he'd taken to the gate. And all along the way, he heard the same chorus of No Statement Given and Still Awaiting Signs, over and over, in the exact same serious-journalist cadences, like the droning of zombies.

Meanwhile, upstairs, the Keeleys were carefully avoiding any of the transmissions from the front of their house, and had turned on Jay Leno instead. The television provided a pleasantly tinny background noise to their activity: packing, wordlessly and quickly, for their journey.

After a commercial break, Leno himself reappeared, looking uncharacteristically grave. "There have," he said, "been a lot of tasteless jokes about the death of Senator Eli Jackson." Just to be safe, Keeley grabbed the remote control; then he watched as Leno sat back and broke into a grin. "And now here's another one!"

The senator pressed a button; the screen went blank.

He stood for a moment, pursing his lips, then went to the window of the far wall and opened it.

Mrs. Keeley, just finishing packing a small overnight case, looked up and caught sight of him straddling the window ledge. She shrieked. "Kevin, no!"

"Ssh," he admonished her, his finger pressed against his lips. "I'm just going down the ladder. I can't face the press tonight. Tell the driver to come around and stop outside the orchard."

She dashed over to him and grabbed his arm. "You can't do that! I don't want to go out there alone!"

He patted her hand. "You won't be alone, Louise. You'll have Barbara. And it's not *you* they're after."

"Yes, I know," said Mrs. Keeley, still trying to pull him in. "But—but I—"

It was at this unfortunate juncture that Barbara entered, and, seeing her parents grappling at the window, her father ready to fall to his death, she screamed, *"Daddy!"*

Senator Keeley flinched at the noise. "Please! Shut up!" he said, his voice low. "I'm just trying to get out the back way. The ladder's still here."

Mrs. Keeley refused to release his arm. "Didn't we decide that you were going to announce Barbara's wedding to the Coleman boy?"

He shook his head. "I've changed my mind. I won't do that without meeting them. What if I announce it, then they decide to pull out, because of our scandal? It would only make things worse. Now let go of my coat. I'll meet you in the car."

He swung his other leg over the sill and started down the ladder.

Careful, he encouraged himself as he descended the rungs; careful, now. *Mustn't make any noises that might attract—*

Lights suddenly blared to life, pinning him to the wall as though he were an insect. Startled, he gripped the ladder and looked over his shoulder.

Through the blinding floods, he could just make out two camera crews, four or five reporters, and a few tailored newscasters. Before he could decide how to react, a boom mike appeared in the air, not far from him.

A newswoman approached, her hand on her ear, a microphone suspended before her chin. ". . . and—yes," she said brightly. "It's Senator Keeley, just leaving his house." She lifted her head and called up to him. "Senator Keeley . . . Senator Keeley . . ."

This was like the whistle that drew forth the dogs. Suddenly she was surrounded by the rest of the newcasters, each of whom shouted his or her own query up at him.

"Senator Keeley, do you think this will cost you votes?"

"Senator Keeley, what's the future of the Coalition for Moral Order now?"

"Senator Keeley, what happened at this morning's meeting with Senator Dole?"

"Senator Keeley, what about the rumors that Senator Jackson was on Lithium?"

"Senator Keeley . . ."

"Senator Keeley . . ."

"Senator *Keeley* . . ."

As the questions continued, overlapping until they sounded like some dissonant, postmodern choral piece, more reporters and cameras appeared from the front of the house, racing to where the action was like hyenas to carrion. And none of the growing multitude, bumping each other into the orchard, seemed to pay any heed at all to the fact that their quarry was perched above them on a ladder.

Well, he could match them absurdity for absurdity, if that's what it took. They wanted a statement? He'd give them one—a magisterial one, delivered with the full force of his authority from sixteen feet in the air, pressed against his cedar siding.

"Gentlemen . . . and ladies," he began. "I am, as are all my colleagues, Republican and Democrat, liberal and conservative alike, stunned and saddened by the circumstances surrounding the death of Senator Jackson—as well as by the death itself. My family and I are leaving town for a few days . . . for reasons I cannot—uh—I mean, to plan an event . . . an event which I cannot . . ." He was slipping up here; better trot out more flouncy rhetoric. ". . . which may heal some of the . . . bad things that Senator Jackson's demise has made us all—uh . . . um . . ." Come *on.* ". . . feel." He winced; it hadn't gone quite as he'd hoped. Why hadn't he prepared for this?

Again, the cacophony from below.

"What's the event?"

"Will you be back in time to attend Senator Jackson's funeral?"

"What's the *event,* Senator?"

"Senator *Keeley* . . ."

Harry Radman, suddenly making himself stand out from the rest, bellowed out, *"Where are you and your family going, Senator Keeley?"*

"Where? To our—farm." He cleared his throat. "And that's all I'm going to say for now."

As the senator climbed back into the house, there was a flurry of confused activity on the ground below. People didn't know if they should wait here, return to the front of the house, or go with the story as is.

Only Harry Radman stood stock-still, a serene smile spreading over his jowly face.

Chapter

fourteen

The sun was large and low over the horizon, a smear of last-ditch, oxidized orange that you could look at without fear. It was the time of day when the denizens of night rose and stretched and prepared for their hours of sovereignty.

The waiters at The Birdcage were just finishing the table setups, and Albert, already in full costume and makeup, was doing a sound check with Celsius, who had eschewed gum for this occasion. As Albert wailed and Celsius twirled, an occasional extraneous performer would flit across the stage behind them, on her way to somewhere terribly urgently.

Armand was behind the bar, moodily downing his first glass of wine. As he sipped, a burly, undershirted, middle-aged Italian—Tony, by name—approached, carrying a keg of beer with what reserve of strength Armand couldn't even conceive. He set the keg behind the bar, and Armand got a sudden whiff of the fermented hops. He wrinkled up his nose, stepped back, and said, "God, that smell!"

Tony mopped his brow and said, "I'm gonna make you like beer some day, Armand."

Armand shook his head in distaste. "You'd have better luck getting me to like football. Or women."

He laughed, then turned and hollered, "Chuck! The club'll be open in five minutes! Let's have that other keg!"

From outside, a youthful voice called back, "Be right there, Pop. I'm inflating my shoe."

Tony shook his head and leaned against the bar. "I could just kill him. Why did I get him those shoes?"

Armand, perhaps more bitterly than he'd intended, said, "Because he's young and ruthless and you're weak and guilty, and he knows all the buttons to press."

Tony, a little stunned by the accuracy of this remark, paused a moment to let it sink in. "Jesus, you're right." He slammed his fist onto the counter, causing Armand's glass to do a little jump. Armand picked it up at once and held it close to him. "If that little punk wasn't getting an athletic scholarship," Tony said, "I'd rip those shoes off his feet."

Armand brightened. "You didn't tell me the scholarship came through! That's wonderful!"

He beamed. "Yeah—*three* colleges." Paternal pride overwhelmed him, and he shrugged wonderingly. "Well, you know, kid's got talent. I don't know *where* he got it . . ."

Armand, his bitterness toward Val now evaporating, chimed in. "I know, it's amazing. Val's getting a degree in engineering—top twenty in his class—and I don't know how Velcro works."

"That's great," said Tony admiringly. "Top twenty—great!" He shook his head, then took a cigarette from a pack in his back pocket and lit up. "Funny, isn't it? When I was born, my father wanted me to be president. When

Chuck was born, I thought, if he doesn't get hooked on drugs or turn gay, I'm fine." He suddenly blanched, then turned to Armand and said, "No offense."

Armand furrowed his brow. "*I'm* not hooked on drugs," he deadpanned. Tony laughed again, and Armand, smiling at how easily he put these potential bully boys at their ease, continued. "In all seriousness, I thought the exact same thing when Val was born. I wanted things to be—you know. Easier for him."

Tony nodded soberly and took a long puff. "Of course," he said, exhaling. "Hey—everybody's a coward when it comes to their kids." He reached a steel-cable arm across the bar and slapped Armand on the back. Armand thought he felt something internal come undone. "But they all turned out all right, didn't they? They lived, they're in college, and they're driving us crazy." Before Armand could add his vigorous assent to this last sentiment, Tony turned and barked, "Hey, don't you have any sense of time?"

Armand peeked around Tony's bus-broad shoulders and saw that this was addressed to Chuck, Tony's son, who had just entered carrying the second keg with, if anything, even greater ease than his old man had. Armand looked admiringly at the boy's straining biceps and back muscles, and the flush in his milk-white cheeks, and, feeling a bit faint, took a fortifying swallow of wine.

Then, as Tony exited, still berating Chuck, Armand returned his attention to the stage, from which the performers had now cleared way. At that moment, a gentle rumba rhythm was piped in over the speakers. Armand checked his watch, then nodded to one of the waiters, who opened the doors to let in the evening's customers.

As they filed in, Armand smiled and greeted them, until he saw Agador slink across the club in a French maid's outfit and fishnet stockings. He slipped backstage, and Armand bolted after him.

He dove through the curtains and nearly toppled Cyril, who was, as usual, in the midst of a small nervous breakdown over the costumes and wigs. "Armand," he cried, his hands fluttering to his face, "we're almost out of tape! How can I send the girls out there if they're not properly taped? They'll be grotesques!"

Armand shot him a baleful look, and said, "Agador."

Cyril meekly pointed to the stairs.

Armand raced up.

Val was in his room, as he had been all day, rereading an old novel by Shirley Jackson he'd left behind when he packed for school. He heard the flurry of footsteps on the stairs, then turned against the wall and concentrated harder on the book, trying to tune out his ridiculous, intransigent, uncaring father; but it was no good. The voices were too loud.

"Agador!" Armand called out.

Agador was heard from next, in a shrill whine. "What did I do?"

"We're redoing the apartment for tomorrow night, God damn it!"

Val sat up, his eyes brightening. Could he have heard correctly?

Agador said, "I know—for the in-laws, right?"

"Right. Everything over-the-top has to go, and we can start with you. What's with that getup? Didn't I tell you to get yourself a uniform?"

"That's what this is. Except for the shoes; I never wear shoes."

"Get a *butler's* uniform, Agador. *With* shoes."

"I'll look like a fag."

"Maybe, but you'll look like a fag in a uniform." He sighed. "You'll start first thing in the morning. I'll get Albert out of the house early . . . tell him he has to leave for a few days . . .''

Val leapt up and raced to the door.

Agador was pouting. ''Where'm I going to get a butler's uniform? I don't suppose it's in the phone book under 'B'.''

Armand, agitated beyond belief, turned and tugged at the bridge of his nose. ''Oh, *God,* this is going to be hard . . .''

''Pop?'' Val, standing in the door to his room, looked out with wet eyes, and smiled.

''Whoo-hoo, Miss Garbo walks among us again,'' hooted Agador.

Val ignored him and gazed lovingly on his father. ''Thanks,'' he said.

Armand started to melt, then shored up his wounded pride and said, ''Do me a favor, Val—don't talk to me for a while.''

Chapter
fifteen

It was coming on dawn before the Keeleys could safely set out on their drive, and even then, a few straggling cameras rolled as they exited the driveway.

Now, with the sun just making its way over the horizon, like a large pink head peeking up over the bedsheets, the big, black Lincoln was on the highway, cruising at a public-spirited sixty-five miles per hour.

The Keeleys were crammed in the back with Louise's enormous Louis Vuitton overnight bag, with which she could not part. "You'll see," she'd told her husband, who had wanted the monstrous thing in the trunk, "on a long drive, you'll be glad of all the things I brought. Card games, magazines, bottled water, candy . . ." It was this last treasure that provoked the senator's approval, as she knew it would.

Now, however, a half hour into the drive, she'd changed her mind even in the face of her own preparedness. "Kevin, please," she said, as signs for the airport came tantalizingly into view. "Please let's just charter a plane."

The senator, sucking on a chocolate drop, shook his

head. "No. We can't get out of this car. The minute we get out of this car, we'll be spotted."

Mrs. Keeley dug through her bag. "Maybe not. I brought dark sunglasses in case we ran into any glare. Also, some old fishing hats to keep the sun off our noses. And extra scarves for me and Barbara. We can wear those and be—what's the word—incognito?"

Barbara giggled, and when her parents looked at her, she said, "Sorry. Silly old memory. The first time I heard that word, in a movie, I thought it meant something really good. Like, 'She's incog-*neato.*'" They continued to stare at her. She leaned forward and smiled. "You know—*neato?* Like, cool? Groovy?" When they still didn't react, she sat back and sulkily said, "I was four, okay?"

The senator turned back to his wife. "This is not a television police drama, Louise. This is real life. And a grown man in a ratty old fishing hat, dark sunglasses, and a seven-hundred-dollar suit is scarcely going to escape notice. Why not just stick a big red clown nose on my face and have done with it?"

Mrs. Keeley shut her bag and turned angrily to the window. "Fine, then. Let's drive all the way to the South Beach, as planned. Get out there just in time to meet Mr. and Mrs. Coleman with our clothes wrinkled, our hair all matted, and our joints stiff. Perfection. With all they've undoubtedly heard of the notorious, scandal-ridden Keeley family, why *shouldn't* we arrive looking like we've just crawled out of a grave?"

"They're not like that," protested Barbara. "They're not judgmental at all like that. In fact—in fact—"

Her parents looked at her expectantly, awaiting what was to come next.

"Never mind," she said. It was a long, long drive to South Beach; best to deliver the news when it was less easy to turn back. Like, say, when they pulled up at the Goldmans' front door.

The chauffeur took all this in without comment, as was his function. And every so often, he checked his rear-view mirror, where a silver Escort never failed to show up, either directly in back of them, or a car or two behind. Just now it was especially close, and in the growing light of day, the chauffeur could see, as he'd expected he might, that one of the two gentlemen in the car was the largish newsperson who had given him such a tidy wad of cash.

Chapter
sixteen

lbert had been surprised—in fact, astonished—that Armand suggested spending a morning at the beach. So gallant of him . . . so romantic . . . quite like the old Armand, the one he'd fallen for all those years ago. Here they were, in the midst of a family upheaval, and with Albert just having introduced a difficult new number, and Armand suggests the beach! He sat at his vanity and stuck a few tufts of hair beneath his straw sombrero, then checked his reflection, and finally shook his head that he should really be going there. The beach! He might almost fall for Armand all over again.

It was a glorious day, of the kind that has made the South Beach the paradisaical playground of the smart set. And weren't they all here today!—supermodel wannabes in all their glory, sauntering across the sands as if they had about a month and a half to reach the water; buffed, lanky gay boys, bursting out of their trunks and shamelessly holding hands; a bevy of whooping, hand-slapping lesbians in the midst of a high-powered game of volleyball; and pasty-white tourists, gleefully shedding everything except their cameras and basking ecstatically beneath the great, golden Ra. Certainly it was a pagan setting, pagan through and through. And while Albert had only to think of dear Val in a hushed Christian chapel exchanging vows with his bride for his throat to close up with pious emotion, he could not deny that this heathen seaside revelry gave him his truest sense of God. Why didn't they come here more often? How had they let themselves forget? *Dear* Armand . . .

All this spun round in his head, and all he could manage to say was, "Oh, how I *love* the sun!"

He and Armand were sitting contentedly, with the stillness of alligators, beneath a large beach umbrella. Armand was wearing a safari cap and glasses and was reading a Jackie Collins novel. Albert loosened a button on his rayon, long-sleeve chemise and let the lovely heat tickle his throat.

Armand put down his paperback and sighed. "It is glorious, isn't it?" he said. Then, narrowing his eyes at Albert, he said with some concern. "You know, you could *use* some extra sun. Take a few days off . . . you look tired."

The diva in Albert, immortal and ageless, went on immediate alert. "What do you mean?"

"I—nothing." He went back to his book.

Distressed, Albert looked at his arms; there was a certain sallowness to them, it was true. But—tired? Albert? *Starina?*

In some distress, he interrupted Armand's reading. "But you must have meant something."

Armand turned, but kept the book open and in place. "I didn't. I swear." A brief pause. "I just meant you look tired."

Albert hauled himself up onto his knees, and put his hands on his hips. "Tired means 'old.' 'You look tired' means 'You look old.' And 'You look rested' means

'You've had collagen.' " Upset, he began to pack up his beach bag.

"No, no," said Armand with an unconvincing laugh. "You look wonderful! Too good to waste indoors." There was an agitated manner about Armand today; Albert was too angry to wonder what it meant. If he hadn't been, he might have seen Armand take a quick, nervous glance back at the apartment, where, in the window, he could just make out a faint blur of activity.

What he couldn't see was Kiko and Dante (out of costume, of course) busily carrying Albert's wigs out of the bedroom and down the stairs to The Birdcage, while Wilhelmina and Lola (equally boyish today) carefully removed an enormous oil painting of a spectacularly endowed satyr. Directing all this activity was Cyril, who was simultaneously pinning up a pair of black trousers on Agador. Because if Agador was forced to dress as a butler, he was determined at least to be a snugly tailored one.

"Not too short," he commanded Cyril. "I want that Armani buckle in front."

Val appeared from the bathroom, carrying a magazine and looking very distressed. He held the publication at eye level and said, "Who put *Playboy* in the bathroom?"

Kiko raised her hand proudly and said, "Leave it. It's what *they* read."

Val dropped it in a nearby wastebasket, then turned and shook his finger at her—at all of them. "Look, don't add anything. Just subtract. And *hurry*. This place has got to look respectable by six!"

Several dozen yards away, Armand was chasing an indignant Albert across the sands. "Let's go window-shopping," he said enthusiastically.

Albert looked the other way, hurt beyond measure. "No, thank you. I want to go home. My day is ruined."

Armand opened his arms to the sun. "This day? *This* day is ruined? Nonsense!" He tweaked Albert's arm. "Come on, I'll buy you anything you want."

Albert stopped short, then looked at Armand to ascertain how serious he was about this; it was a very un-Armand offer to have made.

Seeing a sort of desperate willingness to please in his eyes, he said, "Well . . . I'll have to change my shoes."

Armand grabbed him by the arm and started leading him in the opposite direction. "Never mind, I'll buy you a pair."

"I have no peds. Armand, why can't we go home? What's going on?"

Armand immediately bridled. "Nothing. I . . . nothing."

He might as well have been wearing a T-shirt that said I AM LYING. Albert sniffed at him, then, more determinedly than ever, made a beeline for their building.

A dozen things to say ran through Armand's head, all designed to stop Albert in his tracks—and of these, Armand, panicking, grasped onto the lamest:

"Oh!—I . . . I've hurt my . . . thing," he said, grabbing his wrist. Then, changing his mind, he started hopping, and said, ". . . ankle."

"Your what?" said Albert, turning back slowly and suspiciously.

"My ankle. Oh!" He grimaced in pain. "I don't think I can make it up the stairs." He leaned against a lamppost and held up one foot, as though it hurt to put pressure on it.

Albert, deciding that Armand wouldn't lie about something so vital as an injury, suddenly turned maternal and consoling. "Do you want to wait here and I'll bring some ice down?"

"No!—No, I . . . just . . . uh, no . . ." He took an

anxious glance up at the apartment windows, but he was too close now; the angle was wrong. He couldn't see what was going on up there.

What was going on, was progress—substantial progress. Most of the ornate, rococo touches that had framed the vast array of nudes and phalluses had been removed, as well as, of course, the nudes and phalluses themselves. Val was just giving the apartment a final walk-through for any remaining decadence he may have missed. Just a few minutes ago, he'd remembered that the light-switch cover in the laundry room was imprinted with an image of Michelangelo's David, with the switch protruding where the penis should have been; he was still trying to locate a screwdriver to remove that. As he passed into the entrance hall, he almost bumped into Dante and Beatrice, who were carrying an enormous moose head through the door.

Val was nearly apoplectic. "Wh—what's *that?*"

Beatrice giggled and gave the moose's snout a kiss. "Isn't it a scream? From the antiques shop down the street." Noticing Val's rapidly reddening face, she frowned and said, "Too butch?"

Through gritted teeth, Val said, "Don't *add!*"

The girls stood for a moment, mortified by this lack of appreciation of their creativity; then, from behind them, Albert's voice came wafting up the stairs. "—wish you'd stop blocking my way, Armand."

Armand's voice followed, at full bellow; he was clearly trying to warn those above. *"I'm sorry! I can't walk any faster . . ."*

Val and the girls stood frozen in horror for a moment, then Val hissed, "Put the moose in my room!" When they stared into the apartment in confusion, he pointed out the door down the hallway. "In *my* room."

They scooted away, the moose head wobbling dangerously between them. Val followed, directing Cyril and the other girls to the door to the club. "Downstairs! Now!" he commanded them in a stage whisper, as he opened the door and stood by it, waiting.

"But—but we're not quite finished yet," Cyril protested as he folded up Agador's pants. "What's the matter?"

"Albert's coming up the front stairs," Val explained, and Cyril needed to hear nothing more; he virtually teleported himself downstairs, wanting to be well out of the way of the ugly scene to follow.

Agador, now in his underwear, reappeared at the top of the stairs, having fought the flow of traffic all the way up. "What's going on?" he asked.

"Go back down, *now*," Val snarled at him. "Hurry!"

Agador gave him an I-don't-think-so look, then put his hands on his hips and said, "Your sire hired me, your sire can fire me, and in between, only *he* can boss me— not you, sweet-cheeks. I *can*, however, do favors for you, the last of which I ever do is this." He held out one hand, swinging a screwdriver from between his thumb and forefinger.

Val snatched the screwdriver and put it in his pocket, then was about to shove Agador back through the club door, when he heard the noise on the front stairs reach the landing before the door. Not wanting to risk a noisy fight, he said to Agador, "Fine, stay—but *hide*." Agador, stunned and delighted by this intrigue, dove behind a divan.

Val shut the door tight, ran to the foyer, and pressed himself against a wall, awaiting Albert's entrance with trembling terror.

By this time, Albert had just managed to get the increasingly gimpy Armand to the door. Just as he was about to turn the handle and let them in, Armand went completely limp, his deadweight almost pulling Albert to the floor. *"Ohhh,"* he moaned, "I really think I need a doctor . . ."

Albert sniffed. "Don't be silly." He hoisted Armand back up; Armand tended to forget how strong Albert could be. He gently whisked up Armand's pant leg and examined the ankle. "It isn't even swollen. Here." He reached out, flung open the door to the apartment, and lugged Armand inside.

Val was there, huddled into a corner and smiling sheepishly. What was wrong with the boy? "Vallie, dear," Albert said with crisp authority, "don't just stand there looking swoony. Help me get your father into a chai—" At that moment, he took in the rest of the apartment, screamed, and let Armand drop heavily.

"Oof," said Armand, getting back to his feet. "What is it?"

Albert's hands clasped his face as he surveyed the emptiness before him. "We've been robbed!"

Val, desperately trying to dampen the coming firestorm, said, "No, Albie, we . . . I've just taken a few things out. They'll all—they'll all be in place by the time you get back."

Albert looked at him completely uncomprehendingly. *"Back?* Where am I going?"

Val turned to Armand, who was wiping the creases from his pants. "You didn't tell him?"

Albert whirled on Armand. "What? Tell me what?"

Armand stood to his full height, no longer feigning limpness. He took a deep breath and said, "Val's fiancée is coming tonight. With her parents. And we . . ." He stole a glance at Val for moral support. ". . . we thought . . . it might be better if you weren't here."

A terrible pause followed—a pause in which whole galaxies could have perished in flame, and perhaps did.

Then, with ferocious stillness, Albert said, "I see." He lowered himself grandly into the chair he had originally intended for injured Armand. Then, again, he said, "I see."

Val felt as though he might evaporate from shame. "It's just for tonight," he said in a pathetic, pleading voice.

Albert bit his lip and turned away from him—away from them all. "I understand," he said, as majestic in his suffering as ever Greer Garson was. "It's just while people are here. It's all right, my darling. It's nothing. It's painful, but it's not important. I'm leaving. The monster. The monster is leaving. You're safe."

He rose and walked out the front door in the exact manner in which Mary, Queen of Scots must have walked to her execution.

After a moment of silence, Armand turned to Val and said, brightly, "That went well!" Then he winked and dashed out the door after Albert.

Val stood at the door, still too emotionally wound up to move. Dante and Beatrice reappeared from his bedroom, still carrying the moose head, and Agador crawled out from behind the divan.

They all stared at the front door for a few moments, as though in anticipation of some kind of aftershock. When none came, Agador clapped his hands and said, "Well, then!" He raised an eyebrow to Val. "Shall I order lunch?"

Chapter
seventeen

———————

lbert's mind was all awhirl. He had every intention, every intention in the world, of marching right out of the building and on into the ocean, on until the water covered his head and filled his lungs and brought his life to a swift and elemental end. And yet as he descended the stairs, he kept waiting for the sounds of someone—of Armand—clambering down the stairs after him, to stop him.

Not that he could be stopped. Not that he would consent to live with this mortification on his soul. A swift, poetic death was the only thing left for him.

Damn him, though; why *was* Armand tarrying?

He had reached the building's vestibule and was ready to step outside, and still no sounds of pursuit. He was beginning to think he might actually have to start striding across the beach like some melodramatic idiot.

Then—finally!—Armand's footsteps, tripping daintily after him. He paused at the front door, readopted his air of mortally wounded dignity, then opened the door before him and went out into the world for the last, the very last time.

Once he knew Armand was following him, he quickened his pace, and gave furious chase before Armand—who was a little too fond of his wine and pastries—could catch up to him, huffing and puffing like a landed blowfish. Quite a scene they'd caused—two fancy, middle-aged men in chase, one in tears, the other in supplication, sweeping past outdoor cafés and open-air markets to the complete atonishment of all who saw them.

When Armand was close enough to place a sweaty hand on Albert's shoulder, Albert whirled and shrieked, "Go away! I hate you! I never want to see you again!" Then, with the sudden relief of so much pent-up anguish, came the inevitable plummet into sobs. "My heart is breaking," he bawled through his hands.

Armand hopped about like an especially anxious manservant. "Oh, God—please. Don't cry. It's all right. You can stay."

Albert's hackles raised up at this condescension, and he turned away. "No," he said, tears suddenly over. "I don't want to stay where I'm not wanted, where I can be thrown out on a whim, without legal rights . . ."

"I have the palimony papers at home," Armand said.

This took the wind right out of Albert's sails. His jaw dropped. "You're lying," he said; then he staggered back a few steps. Armand reached out and grabbed his arm, steadying him. Across the street, a group of teenagers broke into open laughter, and pointed at them. Albert barely noticed. "This is too much for me," he said, trying to touch his forehead with one fluttering hand. "Too much ugliness, too much pain. Here, feel my pulse. Am I all right?"

Armand placed his two forefingers on Armand's wrist, then, after a slight pause, began stroking him consolingly. "My goodness," he said. "It's *very* fast. Let's get you out of the sun."

He led him toward one of the umbrella-topped tables at a nearby café. At their approach, several of the diners who had been openly observing them turned and affected not to have noticed them at all.

While Armand was sliding a chair under Albert, a waiter hurried over to them. Before he could even come to a stop, Armand said, "Water. Right away," and he turned on his heel and was gone again.

Armand sat down and faced Albert, who looked ashen.

"It's the end," said Albert, looking down into his lap. "It's the end, I know it is."

"Just be still. Breathe, breathe . . ."

"Oh, what I'd give for a Pirin tablet! . . ."

The waiter flew back to the table, carrying a pitcher and two glasses. He set these before Armand, who nodded and said, "Thank you. And the usual."

"Right away, Señor Goldman."

Albert looked up and realized he was in the Café Parezi, not more than a block and a half from the club. That desperate flight across town, Armand at his heels—only a *block and a half?* How trauma elongated time—!

He was momentarily so astonished by this, that he sat quietly as Armand dipped a napkin into his water and held it at the back of his neck. At the touch of the napkin, he recalled himself to the moment, sighed, and said, "That's better."

"Listen, this is not because of *you*. This is because this girl's parents are assholes. Val is *crazy* about you." He dipped the napkin in ice water again and reapplied it to Albert's neck.

"Is he? Oh, that helps. Oh, you're sweet. That water is so cool." He took a sip of his own water and collected himself. Now that he'd played his scene, he was finding that this gentle consideration—the reassurances, the daubing with the napkin—had sapped his will to martyr-dom. He was actually even beginning to see things Armand's way. "Maybe . . . maybe it *is* too much to introduce me as his mother on the first visit. Could you tell him I was a relative who dropped in? Val's uncle? Uncle Al?"

The napkin stopped: Armand was looking at him dubiously. "Well—what's the point? Then you'll be Val's gay uncle Al."

Albert pursed his lips. "I could play it straight."

Armand scoffed at him. "Oh, please. Look at you. Look at how you're holding your glass." Albert did so, and noticed to his surprise that his pinky was extended outward, as though waving at a passerby. "Look at your posture." He took a wider view of himself, and saw that he was sitting at the end of his chair, one hand in his lap, ankles crossed daintily beneath him—something like the posture of Queen Elizabeth II opening Parliament.

"What's wrong with how I'm sitting?" he asked, defensively. "Children go to special schools to learn to sit like this!"

"Yes—*girl* children. *Finishing* schools. My point exactly." Armand sat back as if to say, Here endeth the discussion.

But Albert wasn't giving up. He deliberately drew in his pinky, then said, "And what about you? You're obviously not a cultural—whatever it is. You've never been to a museum and you eat like a pig."

"Albert, these people are right-wing conservatives. They don't care if you've been to a museum; they care if you golf. And they don't care if you're a pig. They just care if you're a fag."

The waiter flitted over to them again, bearing two club sandwiches. "Right away, as ordered, sir!" he said proudly. And just as quickly, he was off again.

Albert sat staring down at the sandwich, not really seeing it yet. His shoulders began to sag. He heaved a melancholy sigh.

Armand, confronted with this, the result of his victory, felt his heart crack in two. What was he doing? This was *Albert*—Albert, the sun and the moon and the . . . the whatever else the songs say. He reached over and placed his hand on Albert's. "Oh, fuck 'em!" he said, grinning crookedly. "Of *course* you can pass as an uncle. You're a great performer. And I'm a great director! Together we can do"—a brief flash of self-doubt—"*almost* anything."

Albert brightened immediately; trauma passed through him as though through a sieve. "Oh, Armand! Really?"

"Absolutely. We have"—he checked his watch—"five hours. Let's get started. First, your pinky."

"What about my pinky?" he said, darting his eyes to it—too late.

"It's up again," said Armand. "Get it down. And don't lean forward so—sit up straight!" He reached over and slapped Albert on the back.

Albert reeled from this as from a kind of assault. "Oh!—my God! Are you crazy?" He held his arms up to protect himself, in case Armand hit him again. "What are you doing?"

"Stop whining. I'm teaching you to be a man." A woman at a nearby table, hearing this, rolled her eyes at her friend and whispered, *"Those who can't do . . ."*

Armand pulled his chair into place before his sandwich. "Now, this is a dinner party, so let's work with the food. Spread some mustard on that bread. Not with the spoon! And don't dribble little dots of mustard on. Take the knife and *smear*." He took the top off his sandwich and demonstrated for poor, fumbling Albert. "Men *smear*, Albert." And get that goddamned pinky down!"

He slathered great gobs of mustard across his toasted bread. "Your fingers are iron—*visualize* it. Stop trembling! Hold the knife boldly! With *strength.*"

Albert tried to do as Armand did, but lost control. "Oh, God!" he shrieked. "I've pierced the toast!"

"So what? The important thing is not to go to pieces when it happens. React the way a man would. Calmly. Just say to yourself, 'Albert, you pierced the toast. So? Your life isn't over.' Try another one."

Suddenly, Albert felt as though he were on the verge of discovering a whole new way of living. "You're right, you're right," he said, putting down the knife and staring admiringly at Armand. "There's no need to get hysterical. All I have to remember is that I can always get more toast!"

Armand grinned at him. "That's the spirit! Now let's see you walk."

"Holding the sandwich?"

"It—it doesn't matter. Just walk."

After a moment of indecision, Albert put the sandwich down, rose, and crossed the café. A pair of twins at a family table stared at him openly; they'd clearly never seen anything like him before. He walked as though carrying a raw egg between his thighs.

He turned and saw Armand shaking his head in disapproval. "Too swishy?" he asked.

Armand thought for a moment. "Let me give you an image. A cliché, but an image. John Wayne."

"John Wayne?"

"You're a fan. I've seen you glued to those movies."

"For Maureen O'Hara!"

"Whatever the reason—you've seen enough of him to know. He had a very distinctive walk, very easy to imitate, and if *anyone* was a man. . . . Well, try it. Just get off your horse and head for the saloon. Come on."

the birdcage

The young twins grew absolutely rapt as Albert aped dismounting from a saddle—he actually looked more like Margot Fonteyn in recital—then ambled over to Armand, his knees together, his hips shifting.

When he reached the table, he said, seeing Armand's blank face, "No good?"

"Actually . . . it's perfect." He shrugged. "I just never realized John Wayne walked like that."

Albert smiled brilliantly, then turned his chair backward and straddled it manfully. "I'll have a daiquiri, please."

Armand frowned. "Albert, for God's sake, it's the middle of the afternoon."

"No, no," he said in a stage whisper; "I just walked into the saloon, remember? I'm ordering!"

Armand said, "Ah!" and got back into the spirit of the exercise. "Well, then, let's do it right." Adopting a gruff, bartender-like demeanor, he leaned forward and said, "How'd you like a fistful of red-eye?"

Albert flinched and put his hands before his face. "Oh, no, don't hit me again!"

Chapter
eighteen

Senator Keeley was wearing his old fishing hat and a pair of dark sunglasses. Damn Louise and her ideas—especially when she was right. He had taken over the wheel from the exhausted driver, because he didn't want to stop for rest; best to barrel on through.

He peeked into the rearview mirror. Louise and Barbara were huddled together at one end of the backseat, to avoid making contact with the driver, who had slumped into something of a sprawl while sleeping.

He looked at Louise's gaunt, anxious face. Good woman, Louise. A bit hardheaded and contrary at times, but basically a good woman. Stood by him. Never looked back. Never said, Why'd you get involved with that Senator Jackson didn't I warn you not to. Never a reproach. He valued that. A real asset.

And Barbara; no anxiety on her face. Just annoyance. Her mother's looks, her father's courage. She kept tugging at her hair—a nervous habit she'd had since childhood. Tugging, tugging. Tried everything to get her to stop it. Bribes—money, parties. Punishments. Deprivations. Then she started biting her fingernails, and he and Louise decided the hair tugging wasn't so bad.

What kind of a boy, this Coleman kid? Good enough for Barbara? Louise had latched onto the idea of a wedding like a barnacle, because she was ashamed—ashamed to be associated with Jackson. But was a wedding really the answer? Yes, if it was the right kind of family. From the right set. But this Coleman—a cultural attaché. What the hell did that mean? It sounded too—Continental. Too Eurotrash. What if the wife was actually Greek? Some suntanned Athenian socialite with lots of gold bracelets and no brassiere? Or what if Coleman himself was the one with the gold bracelets? A thin, greased-hair pleasure boater of some kind? Always champagne-popping? This could be a disaster; Louise just didn't realize it. That's why it was so important to get there as soon as possible. Judge the situation after he'd seen the parents. If they were as bad as he feared, he could talk Barbara out of it—no, no, he'd never be able to do that; but he could talk her into a wait. A year-long engagement. Offer her bribes again. A house in Georgetown. A new car. Something like that.

He took another look at Barbara and thought, Nah. Never work.

Damn Jackson anyway. Everything happening so fast, he hadn't had time to properly consider the bastard hypocrite who got him into this mess. All his talk about the decay of Christian standards of behavior in this country, the inexorable slide of morality into degeneracy, all his talk of Keeley we've got to dig in our heels and haul this country back to *God*, when all the time, *all the time,* he'd been leading a double life. Got Keeley to put his reputation—and his career, and his family—on the line, then gambols off to play hide the salami with an underage ethnic. Keeley wished Jackson were still alive, just so he could kill him. Why, the thought of the craggy-faced, homily-spouting asshole made him mad enough to—

Wait a minute. Here was the exit.

"Jesus Christ!" said Fishburn, Harry Radman's driver and photographer, as the senator's car skidded across two lanes and onto the ramp marked to I-95 SOUTH. Harry Radman held onto his seat for dear life as Fishburn attempted the same maniac maneuver, to a chorus of irate car horns.

Radman shut his eyes tight in anticipation of a crunch, but heard nothing. Then, feeling the wheels once again moving smoothly beneath him, he opened his eyes. The senator's car was still in front of them, going about seventy-five.

"Guy's a fucking maniac," said Fishburn, wiping his forehead with a Wendy's napkin, taken from a stash he kept between the seats.

Harry Radman peered ahead at the senator's car, and started idly picking up the Doritos that had spilled into his lap during the swerve and popping them into his mouth. "Yeah," he said, his brow furrowed. "Wonder what the hell's so important in South Beach?"

Chapter

nineteen

---

armand had stripped down to his sleeveless T-shirt and was standing under a tree, pretending to read a newspaper with one hand tucked under his arm.

Albert, also carrying a newspaper, lurched toward him, executed a flamboyantly overdone double take at the sight of him, then extended his hand. "Armand Goldman!" he said. "You old so-and-so. How about those Dolphins?" When Armand merely stared in reply, he grimaced and said, "Screaming fag?"

Armand bit of a sarcastic reply, then said, "Here. Stick your hand our sideways, not palm down." He twisted Albert's arm into the proper position. "I'm going to shake it, not kiss it. And tighten that wrist. No, straighten it and *then* tighten it." He surveyed the finished product; Albert held the arm in place with a look of terror on his face, lest he move and ruin the pose. "Better," said Armand, nodding. Then he stepped back, smiled, and in a deep, gregarious voice, said, "Al! You old so-and-so!"

Albert withdrew his hand. "I just said that!"

"Well, now I'm *saying* it. *Al!*" He grabbed Albert's

hand and shook it vigorously; Albert emitted a tiny shriek of alarm, then regained his composure.

"Armand, you old sod," he said, deepening his voice, "you old spotted dog, you old black worm, you."

Armand frowned. *"Black worm?"*

Albert shrugged. "I heard it in a movie once." Armand continued to stare at him. "It was British." Still no response. "I'm new at this! Stop being so hard on me!"

Armand shrugged, then resumed his role-playing. He hit Albert in the shoulder with the newspaper, and said, "So, Al, old man, how do you feel about that call today? A fourth-and-three play from the Dolphins with only sixty-four seconds left."

Albert squinted his eyes. "You don't even know what that means, do you?"

Armand gritted his teeth. "It doesn't matter. For God's sake, just play along. Now, *how* do you *feel* about that *play*, Al?"

"How do you think I feel. Betrayed. Bewildered . . ." He sighed in resignation, then looked at Armand, whose mouth was hanging slack. "Wrong response?"

Armand shook his head. "I'm not . . . sure." He wiped a film of sweat from his forehead onto his wrist. "We'd better take it from the top."

Albert giggled and hopped up and down. "This is very exciting!"

"Yes—yes it is . . . *fella.*" He gave Albert a mock punch in the jaw, then motioned him to back up to his starting position. "Damn right. Fuckin' *A* right! Swing that by me again, compadre!"

Albert, giddy with excitement, backed up right into a beefy young man in pink shorts who was sitting on the grass with a friend.

"Hey!" the man exclaimed, fending off Albert's thighs and tush.

Albert leapt away, then turned and held his face in hands. "Oh, my word! I'm so very sorry!"

"Just take it easy, will ya?" the man said, repositioning himself closer to his friend.

Armand strode over to him manfully. "*You* take it easy, pilgrim," he said, in a voice just a hair lighter than Arnold Schwarzenegger's.

The young man eyed him with astonishment for a moment—this gray-haired, middle-aged man in a T-shirt and gold chains—then gave his friend a Do-you-believe-this look and turned back. "Well, *he* bumped into *me*."

"Well, tough gazongas." Armand ground his heels into the dirt and clenched his fists.

The young man shook his head and chuckled. "Listen, pal, why are you being such a prick?"

"Why are you being such an asshole?"

Albert emitted a little squeal of fear.

The young man rose to his very full height.

"Did you just call me an asshole?" he asked, no trace of amusement left in his voice.

Armand, realizing he was well into it now, inadvertently got himself in deeper by saying. "No . . . actually, I was talking to the asshole behind you."

The asshole behind him, it turned out, was even taller.

Chapter
twenty

The swelling had begun in earnest by the time Albert got Armand back to the apartment.

"Here," he said as he placed a cold compress against Armand's face and pressed his hand over it to keep it in place. "Hold that. Keep it from getting any worse. Don't want my knight in shining armor to suffer any horrible disfigurement!" He stood up and regarded Armand, stretched out miserably on the couch. "You were magnificent!" he said, clasping his hands beneath his chin. "Marvelous! *Very* masculine. I'm so proud of you. That big idiot looked so ridiculous when he sat on you and banged your head on the ground."

"I wouldn't know," murmured Armand. "I didn't have the best view of him."

Albert clicked his tongue. "He didn't even know how to box!"

Armand swallowed with some difficulty. "Why did he stop? I thought he'd keep on till he killed me."

Albert looked at his nails with sudden concentration. "Oh. Well. I started to hit him."

Armand turned, wincing in pain with the effort, and said, "You? *You* hit him?"

"Yes. With my hat. Repeatedly." He shrugged. "Didn't do very much good at first. But then he started laughing so hard, I guess all the anger just emptied out of him. He and his friend just up and left." He rolled his eyes. "Back to the Gorilla House at the zoo, I imagine. Let's go next week, and throw peanuts at them."

Val rushed in with a towel, leaving the laundry room door open; the lilting sounds of Agador singing "Vogue" in a high soprano spilled out into the living room.

"Oh, you're a dear, Vallie," said Albert. "I'll go get some ice to put in this. Be right back, love!" He punched Val in the shoulder, lightly, then traipsed off to the kitchen.

Val looked after him in astonishment. "Pop, Albie just hit me in the shoulder!"

Armand shut his eyes. "Well, he's learned *something*."

Agador appeared in the doorway, balancing a load of whites on his hip and vogueing madly; a moment later, he was gone again.

Val crouched down next to Armand. "Can't we hire a straight maid for tonight?"

"There are no straight maids in South Beach." He took the towel from Val and daubed at his bruise. "And I have more bad news for you." He lay back again, and looked Val in the eye. "I told Albert he could stay."

The boy's face fell. "What? *Why?*"

"Why?" Armand felt a little spidery flourish of anger at his son. "Because he said his heart was breaking! Because he's my beloved friend and companion. Because he raised you!"

Val let his head fall back. "Oh, God. What . . . who will we say he is?"

"Your uncle."

"My—" Val considered this for a moment, then laughed and shook his head. "Well, forget it. We might as well forget the whole thing."

"Don't be so negative. You're only twenty years old. Have some hope."

Val got to his feet and started pacing. "Hope? About what? I mean, once they see you and Albert together, it's—oh, God, what a mess."

"Yes," said Armand angrily. "What a mess, to have them see where you came from, who you really are. Horrific."

Val cocked his head at him. "Pop! It's not like you to be sarcastic."

Chastened, Armand sat up, still holding the towel to his face. "What we really need is a woman. We could get away with Albert as an uncle if we had a woman as a mother. Ironic, isn't it? When you *need* a woman . . ." Suddenly, he brightened, dropped the towel, and stood up. "Say. Why don't I just ask your mother?"

Albert, ice bucket in hand, reentered the room just in time to hear this, then hung back to hear what followed.

Val looked a bit stunned. "My . . . mother? She—she wouldn't do it!" He looked at Armand hopefully. "Would she?"

He shrugged. "How do we know?"

"Well, she hasn't seen me in twenty years. That's a pretty good indication."

"No, it isn't! Twenty years ago she was a young girl—scared, broke. But now . . ."

From across the room, Albert chimed in. "It's very unfair of you to try to talk Val into this, Armand. He has every reason not to wa—"

"You really think she'd do it?" asked Val, interrupting him. "Wow. I mean . . ." He shook his head, and with a touch of awe, said, "My *mother*."

Father and son smiled at each other with exhilarating expectation. Albert, forgotten, held the ice bucket over his head, then hurled it to the floor, where it clattered about noisily and scattered ice across the apartment.

Armand and Val spun around and looked at him in alarm.

He glared back at them.

"Oops," he said.

━━━━━━

I s it her?'' Albert asked. "Is she there?"

Armand hushed him with one hand, then swiftly returned it to the steering wheel of the yellow Mercedes. In his other hand, he held a cellular phone. "Katharine?" he said, his voice infused with a kind of forced jubilance. "Katharine Archer? . . . Armand Goldman!"

Albert leaned so far into Armand that he pinned his arm against his body. Armand took the phone away from his face and hissed, "For God's sake, Albert, I can't steer!"

"I just want to listen," whined Albert.

Armand groaned, then switched hands and held the cellular phone between his and Albert's ears.

"Oh, my God! Armand," Albert heard. "I don't believe it! It's been a hundred years. Where are you?"

Armand held the phone closer to his mouth, while Albert pouted and mockingly mouthed the words, *It's been a hundred years.*

"On the road," said Armand happily, ignoring Albert. "I was wondering if I might see you. I have an unusual proposition for you.—What's that? No, no money involved. Money! Who are you talking to about money? Don't you remember how hopeless I am with—" He caught sight of Albert frowning at him, then dropped his voice and said, "I really don't want to say anything more over the phone. I'll be there in five minutes. Sorry about the short notice. Are you available?" Albert leaned into him again, but Armand held the phone away from him this time. ". . . Uh-huh . . . Uh-huh . . ."

Albert plucked at his sleeve. "Stop it! What's she saying!"

". . . Uh-huh . . ." He grinned, then turned even farther away from Albert.

"Stop it, Armand, or I'll honk the horn."

". . . Uh-huh . . ."

"I swear I'll honk it."

"Me, too . . . uh-huh . . ."

Albert reached over and pressed the center of the steering wheel. The horn blared to life. Armand yelped, barked "Bye" into the cellular, then hung up and grabbed the wheel away from Albert, almost sending the car into the opposite lane. Albert grabbed his hat while Armand righted the wheel.

"Are you trying to get us killed?" Armand cried.

Albert shrugged. "Maybe. What did she say?"

"She's going to see me. Why don't I drop you off at a café or something? I'll be back in fifteen minutes."

Albert hugged his arm. "Oh, that's all right! I'll go up with you. I'm sure there's a waiting room."

Armand smiled at him nervously. Now that he'd given up on lessons in masculinity, Albert appeared to have boomeranged in the opposite direction; at the moment he looked something like Greta Garbo in male drag.

They left the car in a self-park garage and took an elevator up to the offices of what Armand was surprised to find was called The Archer Spa. Katharine had clearly done well for herself; but then, that shouldn't surprise him. Any woman with determination enough to bed a gay man was capable of getting anything else she wanted, too.

They found themselves standing before a frosted-glass partition that had etched on it KATHARINE ARCHER, PRESIDENT. Just beyond it sat an impeccably coiffed, spectacularly manicured secretary, who regarded them inquisitively across a white lacquered desk. When they said nothing, she raised an eyebrow at them, and Armand, feeling an implied threat, cleared his throat. "Miss Archer, please. Armand Goldman."

The secretary smiled; clearly, she had been expecting him. "Go right in, Mr. Goldman."

He smiled back, a bit nervously, and began to make his way through another glass door into Katharine's sanctum sanctorum. Then, sensing that Albert was following him, he stopped, paused before the door, and motioned to Albert to take a seat on the chair by the secretary's desk.

"Let me go in with you," Albert whispered. "Please."

"Don't be ridiculous. You'd only be in the way."

"I wouldn't, I'd support you." He checked to make sure the secretary wasn't eavesdropping.

"I don't need any support. Go read a magazine." He pointed sternly to the chair, and Albert was forced to obey.

He sat, crossed his legs daintily, folded his hands in his lap, and held his head aloft, indignantly. He may be forced to sit, but he wouldn't read a magazine; no one could make him read a magazine. Not even Armand.

Armand sighed, then forged ahead into Katharine's office.

When he was gone, Albert stuck his tongue out at the door, checked again to make certain the secretary wasn't watching him, then guiltily picked up a copy of *Men's Fitness* and started paging through it. After four pages of pectorals the size (and presumably the consistency) of hubcaps, he felt faint and had to put the magazine back down.

Meanwhile, Armand had discovered that Katharine's office looked just as she did: streamlined, very modern, very elegant, and very expensive. She rose, all tawny and leonine and unabashedly sexual, and looking very much younger than her forty-whatever years. She gave Armand a smile that made him feel like a long-anticipated luncheon delivery.

"Armand Goldman," she said, as if narrating this scene to an invisible companion. She put her hands on her hips and shook her head.

He said, "Katie Archer," just for symmetry's sake. Then he had a second thought, and said, "Or is it Mrs. Something now?"

"No, I'm between husbands." She flapped a hand at the white leather sofa. "Sit down. My God!" she said, as she lowered herself seductively onto one of its cushions. "I've thought about you so many times . . . every time I saw an ad for The Birdcage. Are you still with Albert?"

He perched himself on the sofa's arm and sat with his hands in his lap, like Little Miss Muffet. "Yes, yes," he said brightly. "Still together. And—and you! You've done very well." He made an expansive gesture, taking in the whole of her fabulous office.

She winked at him. "Because of you. The money you gave me started this place. You should have gotten stock for it."

He shrugged. "I got Val for it. It was a fair trade."

"Is he . . ." She bit her lip. "*How* is he?"

"Fine. He wants to get married."

That was too quick; almost cruelly quick. He could

see the nearly wounded look her face adopted before she could compose herself and banish it. Clearly, she hadn't considered that she might be old enough to have a son who was of marriageable age. "Well!" she said. "How old is he?"

"He's twenty."

"Twenty." She shook her head, and looked off into space. "My God. Twenty years . . ."

"And today," he pressed on, wanting to strike while she was still off-balance, "for the first time, he *really* needs you."

Katharine looked up at Armand, and Armand saw in the face of the powerful businesswoman a glimpse of the guileless gamine he once knew.

Outside, in the waiting area, Albert was busy checking his makeup in his compact mirror. If he positioned the mirror just so, he could catch the secretary occasionally eyeing him. He watched her, waiting for the first hint of disapproval or derision in her manner; then, wouldn't he make a scene that would make Armand regret this awful, crackpot idea! But the secretary only looked amused, not offended.

Suddenly the buzzer on her desk sounded, and a woman's voice issued forth. "Imelda, cancel my appointments for tonight."

"Yes, Miss Archer," said the secretary.

Albert put down his compact and frowned.

Within the office, Katharine clicked off the intercom. Then she looked at Armand and hunched her shoulders. "There. I'm yours."

Armand had by now slipped off the arm and into the sofa proper. "Thank you," he said, humbly.

"It's a pleasure. Really." She went to the wet bar at the far wall of the office. "I normally drink vegetable juice during business hours," she said, opening the refrigerator, "but for this—" She produced a bottle of Veuve Clicquot champagne and two chilled glasses.

He gulped.

She came back to the couch. "Let's drink to Senator Keeley's daughter and our Val." She set the bottle and the glasses on the table. "I'm afraid I haven't done much for him the last twenty years."

"Don't worry about it. Really."

She grimaced as she pried off the champagne cork's wire cage. "I'm not exactly maternal."

"I am. And Albert—" He chuckled. "—Albert is almost a breast."

"Val was lucky, wasn't he?" She put a hand on his. "What time tonight?"

He grinned, and removed his hand. "Six o'clock, to be safe. We'll do a little show for them, and then send them on their way." He took the bottle of champagne from her, and popped the cork. She clapped, as if this had required great skill.

"Do you remember the show we were in when we met?" she said wistfully, as Armand poured for her.

"Yes," he said, topping her glass and filling his own. "Very well." He sang a few phrases—haltingly, and getting some of the words wrong, but with enough élan that she was compelled to join him after a few measures. Carried aloft by the giddiness of the memory, they got to their feet and did a few dance steps together, reconstructing their routine, then dissolved into laughter.

"Ah!" said Armand, gesticulating wildly, "the life of the gypsy!"

"How handsome you were," Katharine said, enticing him back into the dance. "How unavailable. And what a body!"

Armand blushed. "Stop—you're embarrassing me!"

She spun him around, manfully. "You were so terrified! It was so sweet."

"I thought I was going to have a heart attack. I mean, I walk into my room, and there's a *woman* in my bed!"

She leaned into him and whispered, "I paid the doorman twenty dollars. Twenty dollars—in those days!"

He giggled. "And I was so drunk on champagne—I thought, 'What the hell, why not just try it once with a woman and see what the straight guys are raving about?'"

They dipped. "And how long did we last?"

"I don't know exactly." He straightened back up. "From two-thirty to three forty-five A.M."

"Three forty-seven," she said.

"Two times!" he said, astonished.

"Two times for *you*." She smiled wickedly and drew in close. "I, myself, hit double digits."

There's no soap," said Louise Keeley.

"For God's sake," said the senator. "What did you expect?"

"Not very much, but I did expect soap."

"Do you realize where we are?"

"Of course I realize where we are. I'm not an idiot."

"I didn't say you were. Louise! I'm concentrating."

"I realize where we are, but I also realize we are not in medieval Russia. We are in twentieth-century America. I expect soap. At least the liquid kind."

"Please, Louise. This is difficult enough as it is."

"I'm not even looking."

"I can see that."

"Who do you suppose put that hole in the wall anyway?"

"Hooligans. Who else?"

"What am I supposed to do without soap?"

"Go back and wait in the car. I think there are moist towelettes in the driver's compartment."

"I'm not using moist towelettes. I'm not wiping my

hands and face in something synthetic that's been sitting in foil for I don't know how many years."

"It's that or nothing. Look, please go."

"This is scarcely what I expected when you said we were stopping to freshen up for dinner."

"Well, I don't see any luxury hotels around here, do you?"

"*Soap,* Kevin. I don't care about luxury hotels. All I want is *soap.*"

"Look, I'd like not to hear that word anymore. Can we do that? Can we not have that word anymore?"

"What are you wearing?"

"What do you mean, what am I wearing? My suit!"

"What about the blazer I packed for you? More Floridian."

"I don't care. I'm staying in my suit."

"All right, all right. Never mind. I'm sure it'll be fine." She paused. "I can't get this earring in."

"I'm not in a position to help you. *Don't look!*"

"I'm not looking. I'm turning my head to get the earring in. It won't go."

"Do you have another pair?"

"No. Wait!—There it goes."

"Oh, hooray. Is Barbara changing?"

"No. You know teenagers. Casual everywhere. She wore jeans to the Vatican."

"But she's meeting her future in-laws for the first time."

"She's wearing a nice sweater."

"Well, that'll come off. Florida, you know."

"I hadn't thought of that."

"*Don't look!*"

"I wasn't looking. Kevin, honestly, we've been married for twenty-one years."

"Could you just put some paper toweling over the hole?"

"Don't be silly. Pretend I'm not here."

"I can't. It's a pathology."

"Well, this will have to do."

"Blasted hooligans. Who would do such a thing? And why here? What's the point of it?"

"You have to tell me if I look all right. To meet the Colemans, I mean."

"If I'm right about them, we'll be overdressed if I wear socks."

"Please be more positive. For Barbara's sake."

"I'll try. I just hope to God they're not as bad as I imagine."

"I'm biting my tongue, Kevin."

"Are you."

"I'm biting it hard, so I don't say, 'Oh, yes, let's hope they're decent folk like Senator Jackson.' "

"I'm glad you're not saying that. Look, I have to flush now. Will you leave? I'll see you outside."

"Did you shave?"

"No. It'll take me thirty seconds. I brought an electric razor."

"Is there an outlet in the wa—"

"Don't look! Yes. Now *go."*

Louise Keeley left the ladies' rest room and went back to the parking lot, where Barbara and the driver were waiting with the car. She poked her head in the window. "Hi, honey! How do I look?"

"Fine, Mom," said Barbara idly. "Dad ready yet?"

"He still has to shave. Is this the last rest stop before the Florida state line?"

"I think so."

"Ooh! Closer and closer."

Barbara looked suddenly pained. "Yes. Mom, before

114

we get there, can I just tell you quickly that what I said earlier about the Colemans wasn't entirely on the lev—''

Senator Keeley appeared behind his wife, rubbing his face. ''All right, then,'' he said, ''let's get this show on the road. That is, if I've suffered sufficient injury to my dignity today.'' He got back into the car and stared grimly out the window.

As they pulled away, a silver Escort emerged from the opposite end of the parking lot and followed them.

''They changed clothes,'' said Harry Radman. ''Or *she* did, at least. Wonder what for?''

Fishburn chuckled. ''Did you see the toilet paper trailing from the senator's shoe?''

Chapter
twenty-three

———

Val was in his bedroom, standing before a mirror, practicing his smile and extending his hand to the mirror. "Hi," he said brightly. "I'm Val. Mrs. Archer, I'm Val." He nodded his head and tried to look boyish and adorable. "I'm Val . . . Mom." He stood upright, his spine as straight as a piling. "Senator. Mrs. Keeley. Glad to meet you. I'd like to introduce my mother. Mom . . ." He looked at himself, and his shoulders fell. "Oh, God, please. Let this work out."

There was a rap on the door. He turned and saw another one of his father's "girls."

"Uh—hi," he said. "Carmen, isn't it?"

She was wearing a jumpsuit and a turban, which wasn't quite enough to conceal her enormous—and at this proximity, enormously masculine—physicality. She said, "Uh—I'm just looking for Mr. Golden."

"Oh. He's—he's out."

"With Starina?"

"Wi—oh, with Albie. Yes."

Carmen frowned. "Well, thanks."

"Is everything okay?"

She puffed out her cheeks and put her hands on her hips, then lifted two fingers to the bridge of her nose and made a trembling, exhaling sound. "It's just, a girl likes to know where she stands, all right?"

Val went to the door and put a hand on her shoulder. "Of course. Of course she does."

"It's like, almost every night, Cyril says, 'Oh, Carmen, Starina says she won't go on tonight, so be ready.' And I get ready, and what happens? Starina goes on."

"I see," said Val, checking his watch ever so blithely.

"I mean, I need to psyche myself. I need to prepare *mentally* for a performance. I can't just walk on because Miss Queen Bitch of the Universe hasn't been stroked enough."

"Well, I—"

"And if I prepare, I swear to God, it's like—it's like a kind of *death* to have to go back offstage without having done my stuff, just because Miss Fuck-You-World Starina has decided she'll condescend. You know what I mean?"

He drew a breath. "I'm not sure I—"

"So, Cyril just told me. 'Tonight, Carmen, tonight for sure you go on for Starina, 'Cause she's got a sudden other engagement elsewhere.' Now, I've been burned plenty, okay? But I'm a tough old thing. I know not to get my hopes up till I hear it from Mr. Goldman himself. So I took the liberty, you should excuse me for interrupting, of coming up here and inquiring *moi-même.* Okay?"

"Okay, but I—"

"I know, they're out. So poor, secondhand Carmen has to take her chances again, doesn't she?"

Val squeezed her forearm. "Look. I'm sure if Cyril says it's this time for sure, then it's this time for sure. Okay? Carmen?"

She sniffled. "You're little Val, aren't you? All grown up." She batted her eyelashes, suddenly turning on the charm. "I recognize you from your—" she licked her upper lip.—"bedside manner. Quite like the old man. Know just how to talk to a girl." She sidled up to him and rubbed up against him.

He stepped back. "Thanks, Carmen. Listen, I—"

"You know how to treat a lady, that's for sure."

He cocked his head at her. "Well, sure. I've had practice on the genuine article."

Carmen frowned. "Wh—what's that supposed to mean?"

"It means, I'm flattered and everything, but as far as being like my dad—well, only up to a point. I've got a little thing for that extra X chromosome."

Carmen sighed in disappointment. "Never know who you're talkin' to these days."

He laughed. "I have to hear that from *you*?"

She pinched his cheek. "You change your mind, you come lookin' for Carmen, okay?"

"If I change my mind, sure," he said merrily. "But don't hold your breath."

Carmen touched her crotch as she exited. "Honey, taped up like this, all I *can* do is hold it."

Chapter
twenty-four

albert was becoming increasingly impatient. He'd reluctantly gone back to the fitness magazine, and had read a harrowing article on anabolic steroids that he was sure would still be giving him nightmares six months on. After that, he'd gone back to the photos of the bodybuilders at the front of the magazine to check the size of their genital bulges, to see if what the article had said was true. His eyesight had been spotty of late, so he'd been actually nose-deep in a crotch shot when Imelda the secretary started coughing, and it was obvious she was doing so to disguise a laugh. Albert, mortified, threw down the magazine, checked his wristwatch, and commenced a slow boil.

Unaware of the simmering temper outside, Armand, now danced to exhaustion, was half-reclining on Katharine's sofa, a bit the worse for the champagne (he was well into his third glass, and at his age, two was his limit). He felt damp and nervous, but somewhat silly and daring. Katharine had thrown herself on the sofa next to him, rather closer than she could have got away with if she'd just sat politely.

"Phew!" he said, trying to work up the energy to slide away from her. "You're in incredible shape. And you can still dance."

"So can you, Armand. So can you." She dipped a napkin in the ice-filled champagne bucket and touched it to his face.

"Ah, that feels good. Cool."

Without warning, she slipped a hand between the buttons of his shirt and started fondling him. He went rigid as a corpse.

"Where did all this chest hair come from?" she asked wonderingly, as she tugged at it. "Wasn't your chest smooth?"

"I shaved it off for the show. I wanted to look so young . . ." He was really starting to sweat now—worse than during the dancing.

Katharine snuggled up to him and continued petting his chest. "It's so much nicer this way, so much more masculine. All this hair! Let me touch it."

"Funny, Albert says it's beastly; he keeps advising electrolysis."

She tsked, but dared no real criticism of Albert; damn, she was good at this! No wonder Armand had wound up a father. "What a beautiful chain?" she said, as she toyed with Armand's gold medallion. She started unbuttoning his shirt to have a better view of it. "Look how it glitters in that thick, black nest of hair." Armand made some instinctive move to resist, but she pinned him to the couch. "Unbutton your shirt," she growled. "I want to stroke your chest, your beautiful, hairy chest . . ."

"Careful with your nails," he yelped. "This shirt is silk organza. . . . Oh! Look, see? You pulled a thread!"

Suddenly, the door to the office flew open, and Albert stood framed by the doorway like an avenging Fury in some Greek myth.

the birdcage

"I'm sorry, Mrs. Archer," squeaked Imelda from be-hind him. "I couldn't stop him!"

Albert pierced Armand with an accusing gaze, then turned with great dignity and departed.

"Albert!" cried Armand. He leapt to his feet, uncere-moniously dumping Katharine to the floor.

He flew out of the office just in time to see the eleva-tor closing on Albert. "Hold the doors! Hold the doors!" he called out. But Albert looked stonily ahead, as though he hadn't heard a thing; and then he was gone from view, and the elevator began its descent.

Armand groaned, then turned to the startled secre-tary and said, "Where's the stairwell?" She pointed to a door down a small corridor, and Armand dashed over to it, flung it open, and began pounding down the stairs. He'd gone barely two flights down when he realized that Katharine was on the seventeenth floor; then, winded, he buttoned himself up, returned to Katharine's reception area, and without a word to the secretary, called for the second elevator, and took that down to the lobby.

He reached the parking lot just as Albert had slammed himself into the driver's seat of the car and peeled off.

Or, rather, it *sounded* like he was peeling off; but as he sailed regally down the avenue, the sound of squeak-ing and peeling continued, along with the faint odor of distressed rubber.

Chapter
twenty-five

═══════════

by the time Armand got home, the apartment was dark and somber and quiet, rather like a library, or a morgue. He was so accustomed to the place being filled with life—Albert's histrionics, Agador's flutterings, and, lately, Val's anxious tremblings—that it was eerie at first to be greeted by no signs of life.

He went into the living room and found Agador standing on a stack of books, placing a huge crucifix above the mantel.

Armand took one look at the crucifix and silently thanked God that neither of his parents was alive to see this day. "Is Albert here?" he asked.

Agador looked at him strangely. "Isn't he with you?"

"If he was with me, I wouldn't be asking, now, would I? Has he come home, or not?"

Agador, hurt by his tone, pursed his lips and returned to his task. "No."

"Great." He dropped into the sofa. "Then he's driving back from Miami at twenty miles an hour with the parking brake on, and *I* had to take the fucking bus." He sighed, then gestured at the crucifix. "A little monastic, don't you think?"

Agador grinned. "Do you like it? I traded the moose head for it. And they threw in the books. It all goes back tomorrow."

Armand eyed the books. "I haven't heard of any of these. What are they? Nothing ribald, I hope."

"Mysteries?" said Agador, stepping down. "Thrillers."

"Ah. Well. That's high-toned enough. The upper crust love their whodunits."

Val entered the room, carrying a pile of tabloids to be hidden away. "I thought I heard your voice. What happened, Pop? Did you see her? My mother? Is she coming?"

Armand said, "Yes . . . she's coming." He was surprised to find himself feeling a spate of jealousy toward Katharine now; Val was entirely too eager to meet her and fall in love with her. And after Armand had done all the hard work of rearing him!

Val didn't help the situation by flinging all the tabloids into the air. "O-*kay*!" he exulted, as images of Princess Diana, Oprah Winfrey, and Nicole Brown Simpson flapped wildly around his head.

"Ah, there," said a familiar voice from behind them. "You see? It all worked out . . ."

They all turned to see Albert standing in the doorway, backlit, like a 1930s movie queen.

"I'm only here to get my toothbrush," he said, his voice saturated with melodrama. "Agador—will you, dear? It's in the usual place." Agador darted for the bedroom, and Albert stepped inside, into the light. He took an affectionate, tearful look at Val. "How I would have loved to see your children!"

Armand, for whom the bus had been a cruel indignity indeed, stood up and faced him. "Shouldn't you be holding the crucifix?" he asked. "It's *the* prop for martyrs."

Albert took refuge in wounded dignity. "Oh, yes," he said loftily. "Another gibe, another joke at my expense. You were probably laughing at me with Katharine, too. Well, why not?" He opened his arms wide, as if baring his essence to the world. "I'm not young, I'm not new, and everyone laughs at me. I'm quite aware of how ridiculous I am." No one dared respond; this was too naked an admission; shame rouged their cheeks. Albert lowered his head and continued. "And I've been thinking that the only solution is to go where nobody is ridiculous, where everyone is equal." He turned his head slightly toward Armand. "Goodbye, my love."

"Wait!" cried Agador, reappearing with the toothbrush. He handed it to Albert. "Here. I brought floss, too. Mint flavored, like you like. But please, please don't go, Miss Albert."

Albert cupped his hands over the young man's cheek. "My poor Agador. I'm leaving you my stereo . . . all my Dietrich records . . . my red boots . . . and my wigs. My best wigs. I won't need them," he said, turning to stare up into space, "where *I* am going."

Armand had had quite enough. "All right," he said. "I'll bite. *Where* are you going?"

"To Los Copa."

"Los Copa? There isn't anything in Los Copa but a cemetery?"

Albert looked at him knowingly. "That's why I'm packing light."

"Oh, I see," said Armand with disgust. "You're going to the cemetery. With your toothbrush."

"And floss!" interjected Agador.

Albert narrowed his eyes at Armand and said, "Goodbye." Then he turned on his heel and walked out.

Agador fell to his knees in alarm, landing right before the crucifix, like a supplicant. "Miss Albert!" he called.

Armand shook his head. "Shit."

Val put a hand on his shoulder. "It's all right. It'll be better without an uncle."

Better without an uncle. That's what it came down to, for Val, after all the years of mothering Albert had done.

Still, he couldn't quite force himself to be angry at his son. Instead, he turned on his houseboy. "Get up, Agador."

"I'm praying!" he pleaded.

"Well, don't. You have to start dinner—because I have to go after *fucking* Albert."

He left the apartment, slamming the door after him.

Val stared at Agador, suddenly wary. "Can you . . . you *can* cook, right?"

Agador shrugged. "Your father seems to think so."

Chapter
twenty-six

a rmand found Albert sitting on a bench at the bus station, eating from a bag of chocolate schnecken. When Albert saw him pull up, he swiveled his body in the opposite direction.

Armand got out of the car and went to the bench. "Do you mind if I sit down?"

"Yes?" said Albert.

Armand sat anyway. He put his hands in his lap. "You know," he said," my cemetery is in Key Biscayne. It's the prettiest in the world. There are lovely trees, the sky is blue. There are birds. The one at Los Copa is really shit." He leaned back, and observed that Albert was munching faster. "What a pain in the ass you are." Albert stopped munching, his hand suddenly halting while still in the bag. "And it's true: you're not young and you're not new. And you *do* make people laugh. And me—I'm still with you because you make *me* laugh."

Albert lowered the bag to his lap, and sighed.

"So you know what I have to do? I have to sell my plot in Key Biscayne and get a plot beside yours in that shithole, Los Copa, to make sure I never miss a laugh."

He reached into his jacket and produced a sheaf of papers, then passed these over to Albert. "Here."

"What's this?"

"Read it."

Albert took the sheets as though slightly afraid of them, then, turning his head away so that Armand couldn't see him, slipped on a pair of glasses and began to read. After a few moments, he took off the glasses and turned back to Armand. "I don't understand," he said.

"What's so difficult?" He pointed at the papers. "It's the palimony agreement. I told you I had it."

Albert, stunned, threw vanity to the wind and re-donned his glasses. "It—it says here I have the right to give you half of everything I own."

"Yes," said Armand, nodding. "I think it'll be safer if something happens to one of us."

"But," Albert said, almost sputtering in his confusion," who owns it *now*?"

"You do."

Albert felt dizzy for a moment, as if he'd suddenly inhaled a large amount of helium. "You mean, you've given me the club? And the apartment? And *everything*?"

"Yes."

His lower lip crumpled up; then tears streamed forth from his eyes. He shoved the papers back at Armand. "I don't want it."

Armand shrugged. "Then give me half."

"Oh, quick," he said, taking a handkerchief from his pocket and holding it to his nose. "Give me a pen! I don't want all this."

Armand produced a pen from his breast pocket. "Here. Sign it." Albert scrawled his name on the document while Armand held it for him, then heaved a watery sigh. "There," said Armand, putting his hand over Albert's. "We're partners. You legally own half my life and I legally own half of yours."

"But half of the club . . ."

"Don't you think it matters? Take it all! I'm fifty years old and there's one place in the world I call home . . . and that's because you're there. So take it. What difference does it make if I let *you* stay or you let *me* stay?"

"Oh, Armand."

"It's home. It's home for me, and I think, it's home for you, too."

Albert stared into Armand's eyes, willing himself not to melt, and failing. "Of course it's home for me," he said. "Where else?"

Armand patted his hand. "Where else," he said, in confirmation.

Chapter
twenty-seven

Katharine Archer, purse over her shoulder, stood at Imelda's desk and barked into the secretary's phone. "I don't care about flight patterns and sleetstorms in Chicago," she said, "your service promised ten A.M. delivery and the packages just arrived now. Now being four fifteen, eastern standard time. Virtually the end of business hours, am I right?" Behind her, a delivery man tried to sneak onto an open elevator. *"Hey!"* she barked, cupping her hand over the receiver. "You're not going anywhere till this is cleared up."

The delivery man stood rigid in his blue and gold uniform and looked to Imelda for help.

But Imelda had problems of her own. "Miss Archer," she whispered, tugging gently at her boss's sleeve, "the other lines are ringing."

"Go take them from my phone," Katharine hissed. "I can't let this bitch off the hook just yet, or I'll never get through to her again." Imelda bolted from her station to Katharine's office, trembling.

The delivery man, resigned to his fate, sunk into a chair.

"All right, then," said Katharine, pacing with the phone. "This is what I want you to do. First, look up the corporate account number on the shipping receipt. *Just look it up.* I know you have a computer there. . . . Have you got it? Good. Now, maybe there's something that tells you exactly how much I spend on your service each month. . . . There is? Brilliant. Now, listen up, whatever-your-name is . . . Cheryl? Sharon, sorry. Listen up, Sharon. If I am billed for this late shipment, and I mean if you *dare* to send me an invoice of any kind for it, then all of my business goes straight to your competitor from that moment on, which is not to mention the lawsuit you'll have on your hands. I didn't hire you to deliver my packages from Los Angeles. I hired you to deliver my packages from Los Angeles, *by ten A.M.* This was not done. Hence, you've violated our contract, and I don't care that the packages are here now. Now does me no good. Remember this, Sharon: bill me, and the shit hits the fan." She slammed down the receiver, then looked at the delivery man. "Okay, you can go now."

He practically leapt toward the elevator, and pressed the down button repeatedly until the doors opened.

Katharine went back to her office, where she found Imelda madly scribbling onto her pad. "All right, Imelda," she said, "this time I really *am* leaving. Unless that call's important."

"No, Mrs. Archer."

"Put the champagne glasses in the sink for the cleaning service to wash, will you? I'm late. Oh," she said, "and now that the PR kits are here, will you see to it that they're sent out first thing in the morning? In case I'm not in by eight-thirty?"

Imelda looked surprised and dropped the phone to her shoulder. "But, Mrs. Archer, didn't you just tell those express delivery people on the phone that the kits were supposed to go out by noon today?''

''Noon today, noon tomorrow,'' said Katharine with a wiggle of her hand. ''Whatever. The earlier the better, of course, but it's not a crisis. It's also,'' she said, arching an eyebrow, ''none of their fucking business. They broke their contract, and that's the only thing that's important here. Have a good night, now.'' She smiled, winked, and let the door fall shut behind her.

Imelda looked after her, astonished as ever by her sheer bravado. Then the phone rang again, and she leapt to attention. She depressed the flashing button and said, ''Archer Spa, Katharine Archer's office, how may I help you?''

''Katharine Archer, please.'' A man's voice; she recognized it at once as belonging to the man who had visited earlier that day. Mr. Goldman.

''I'm sorry, Mr. Goldman,'' she said, enjoying showing off her cleverness, ''she's left.'' And thank God for it, she thought. ''But she always calls in.''

''Damn,'' muttered Armand, back in the car and speaking on his cellular phone. ''I'd like to leave her a message, then. Will you see that she gets it?''

''Yes, of course,'' said the secretary. ''Go ahead.''

''It's very important. Tell her, 'Don't come tonight.' Just that: Mr. Goldman says, 'Don't come.' ''

''Don't—come,'' the secretary repeated, slowly, as though writing it while saying it.

''Yes. Thank you very much. Good afternoon.'' He clicked off the phone, then looked out the window to where Albert was still sitting primly at the bus stop.

''It's done,'' he called out. *''Come home.''*

Albert smiled brilliantly, then got up from the bench and got into the car.

Chapter

twenty-eight

The chauffeur was back at the wheel, which was all to the good, because Senator Keeley was in no condition to drive. He'd been knocked for a loop by the news story that was coming—no, *spewing*—from the radio.

The senator slumped in the front passenger seat, one hand over his face, and waited for the damned, droning report to end—or, failing that, for the car to pass beyond the range of the station's signal.

". . . and the Reverend Al Sharpton in an interview today said that Senator Jackson's last words—'Your money's on the dresser, Chocolate'—were racist and demeaning. The prostitute's given name is Natumbundra . . ."

Senator Keeley groaned. "That *idiot* Jackson. Now the blacks will start!" Louise reached up, took hold of his arm, and gave it a squeeze. "It's Senator Jackson, not you, dear," she said reassuringly.

"But it's me by association. We were joined at the hip, politically! I only pray the Colemans aren't listening."

"They aren't listening," said Barbara, idly braiding her hair.

"How do you know?" asked the senator.

"Val says they never listen to the news."

He looked at his wife, then back at Barbara. "They never listen to the news, and he's a cultural attaché?"

She looked up from her braid, suddenly realizing she'd blundered. "Uh—well, no. Because—because he has his own people fill him in on events."

"Ah," said Mrs. Keeley.

"You know, to avoid the liberal bias of the news media."

The senator winced. "As if the conservatives are being any kinder about this."

They fell silent for a moment. The voice on the radio regained their attention. "In an exclusive interview with CNN earlier today, Miss Natumbundra revealed that Senator Jackson's fatal heart attack may have been brought on by his extreme excitement over a bondage session he had initiated."

"Oh, good Christ," said the senator, sinking deeper into his seat.

"In her own words, 'Once he had me wrapped up in tin foil and bicycle chains, he started breathing real hard, and he had to sit down for a while before he could continue."

"Tin foil. Bicycle chains. I've had it." He lunged for the radio and switched it off, alarming the chauffeur, who steered wildly into the opposite lane for a moment before regaining control.

Senator Keeley lapsed into a sulk. "You might as well let me out here," he said, in reference to the wooded wilderness through which they were passing. "I'll just find some nice hole where I can curl up and die."

"Nonsense!" Louise said, clutching his shoulder and giving him a good shake. "Remember, Barbara's wedding will disassociate us from all this. Really! The Colemans are a perfect family. They've never even been divorced, have they, Barbara?"

"Uh—no," said Barbara, in a small voice.

"You see? We're on our way to salvation!" As if to echo this, they passed a roadside sign that read MIAMI—80 MILES.

In the car behind them, Harry Radman was still listening to the radio report, laughing wildly while picking at his fingernails with a penknife. Fishburn, at the wheel, was chewing gum obliviously.

". . . Miss Natumbundra is expected to reveal more details of Senator Jackson's final hours when she appears as a guest on the syndicated *Harold Byrne* radio show. Byrne's publicists have announced that Miss Natumbundra will take calls from listeners asking her advice as to which sexual practices she considers safe, and which potentially fatal, in a segment tentatively entitled, and I quote, 'How to Be Kinky Without Kicking.'"

Radman let out a whoop, then shook his penknife at the car in front of him. "Yeah, you run, Keeley," he said merrily. "Go on and run as far as you can. But you sure as hell can't hide!"

Chapter
twenty-nine

———

Val listened to Armand with growing horror. He could feel—actually *feel*—tentacles tightening around his brain.

"It was a question of Albert or your mother," Armand said, his back to his son as he knotted his tie in a mirror. "So I had to choose. And I chose Albert. You understand that, don't you?" He stood back and inspected himself. "Why can't I get this damned tie even?" He flapped the upper half of the tie, which was a good half-inch shorter than the tongue beneath it. "Well, the jacket will cover it." He buttoned himself up and turned to face Val, who was still staring at him in openmouthed disbelief. "I look like my grandfather in this suit," he continued breezily. "He dressed like this in every picture. Killed himself when he was thirty. Any last instructions?"

Val shook his head and dully said, "No. Just . . . just don't talk too much. Don't walk unless you have to. And try not to gesture. It doesn't matter. You sent my mother away. Albert's here. None of this will work."

"It *will*!" he said, clapping the boy on the shoulder.

135

"Don't be so damned negative! I think we can pull this off . . ."

The bedroom door opened, and Albert stood revealed in a severe dark suit. Carefully, he walked in and sat down, betraying not a trace of flamboyance or effeminacy. Then he looked proudly up at Armand and Val, only to discover that they were frowning at him.

"What?" he cried. "No good? Why? I'm dressed just the way you are! I took off all my rings! I'm not wearing makeup! I'm just a 'guy.'"

Armand pointed to Albert's socks. They were bright pink. "What about those?"

"Oh, *those*," cooed Albert, displaying his ankles. "Well, one *does* want a hint of color. Why? What are you thinking? You're thinking dressed this way I'm even more obvious, aren't you? You hate me! I *so* wanted to help you . . . and you both hate me!" He balled his fists and hit his knees, then got up and walked with great masculine aplomb back to the bedroom. He entered, closed the door quietly, and was gone.

Armand shook his head. "You'd think it would be easy, living with Albert. He does all your talking *for* you. If only he didn't always say the wrong thing on your behalf." He sighed, and went after him.

Val stood alone in the foyer, feeling as tragic as Hamlet; tonight was certain to be a disaster. The only question was, a disaster on what scale? Might he and Barbara have to resort to elopement after this? Or would Barbara be shut up in a convent before dawn tomorrow?

Agador came out from the kitchen to begin setting the table. He was dressed impeccably in a dark jacket and long pants—but was completely barefoot. As he lay silverware at each place setting, he swung his hips and sang an old Donna Summer favorite.

Val had to fight back tears. He was already picturing

Barbara in a habit and wimple. "You—you'd better put your shoes on," he said to Agador, knowing it was futile. "It's getting late."

Agador answered in a strange, deep voice that sounded like an over-the-top parody of masculinity. "There's no point in my putting shoes on," he said. "I never wear shoes. They make me fall."

Val shut his eyes. "Go put your shoes on, Agador," he said, trying to remain calm. "And talk in your normal voice. And just . . ." He took a deep breath. ". . . give me a break. *Please*."

Agador must have sensed that the boy was close to the edge, because he unexpectedly said, "All right," and bustled out obediently.

The phone started ringing, jarring Val out of his funk. He glanced toward his father's bedroom; the door was ajar—Armand must be busy trying to cajole Albert into forgiving him.

Val decided that whatever news this call was bringing, he'd better hear it himself first. "Maybe they're dead," he thought exultantly as he dashed over to the phone. Then, spotting the crucifix above the table, he grimaced and said, "You know I didn't mean that. What's *happening* to me?" He stood by the answering machine and waited for it to click on.

Within moments, it did, and a strange woman's voice greeted him. "Armand? This is Katharine. I'm in the car on my way over, but I just got a message telling me not to come tonight, and I wanted to check with y—"

"Hello!" Val cried as he snatched up the receiver. "It's a mistake! He said not to come *late*. I was there."

"Oh, I'm *so* glad. I *thought* my secretary got it wrong. She usually does. I should be there in half an hour." A weighty pause. "Is this . . . Val?"

He felt suddenly tongue-tied. All he could manage was, "Yes."

"Val . . . I want you to know how—how happy I am that I can do this for you. I know it's a little late for . . . you know . . ."

"No. It's fine. Thank you . . . for this." He was suddenly overcome by awkwardness and embarrassment. "See you in half an hour," he burbled, and immediately hung up. ". . . *Mom*," he added softly, once the receiver was back in its cradle.

"What?"

Val turned. Armand had left the bedroom, the door was once again shut. Val quickly turned the phone ringer off.

"Excuse me?" he said.

"I said, What? What did you say?" Armand strode up to him. " 'See you in half an hour—*Mom*?' Was that—"

"Yes," he said with wild defiance. "And there's no way to call her back. She's in her car."

Armand shook his head and laughed, as if the world had gone mad on him. "Are you *crazy*? Albert is totally hysterical *now*. Do you know what he'll do if Katharine walks into this house?"

"Nothing. He won't embarrass me." Armand gave him a dubious look, and he continued. "Pop, I couldn't tell her not to come! She's my *mother*. And she'll make the evening work. I know it. I mean, without her . . ." He shrugged. "I'm screwed. And you know it."

Armand let his shoulders sag in resignation. His head dropped back and he said, "So this is hell." He focused his eyes just above the telephone table. "And there's a crucifix in it."

Chapter
thirty

———————————

To the left, on a gaudy, neon-lit corner, a miniskirted Latina bombshell stormed away from a persistent suitor. He grabbed her arm; she spat a mouthful of obscenities at him, hit him, kicked him, and scratched his face so viciously that he bled. He refused to let go of her, and after she'd spent her fury on him, she fell into his arms and they started to kiss passionately . . .

To the right, at a streetside café, three buffed and suntanned muscle boys sat, shirtless, at a table with a short glass of something clear in front of them. One muscle boy dipped a safety pin into the glass, then shook it dry, and proceeded to pierce the nipple of the muscle boy nearest him. When this young man yelped in pain, the third muscle boy kissed his ear and stroked his neck to soothe him. The first muscle boy inserted a stud into the newly pierced nipple, then turned and called out, "Next." Another shirtless Adonis sat down and proffered his breast . . .

Ahead of them, a filthy man of indeterminate age with a thick, grayish beard and a tattered down vest, crossed the street at a stoplight; but before he could complete the journey, he peered past every windshield and said, "I got mescaline, man. Mescaline, LSD, ecstasy, PCP, man. Heroin? I got heroin. You want heroin, man?" He might have continued had someone from the other side of the street not said," LSD? You got LSD?" thus luring him away . . .

Behind them, two drunken frat boys got into a fight that spilled from the sidewalk into the street, and attracted a throng of hooting, hollering Spring Break celebrants. One of the boys landed a careering punch on the other's jaw, sending him sailing onto the Lincoln's trunk, where he landed noisily before rolling off . . .

And all around them swarmed an army of prostitutes and thieves and pederasts and drunks and lesbians and addicts and advertising professionals—each and every variety of the dregs of humanity.

They came to a stop once again, next to a sign that read NO CRUISING WHEN YELLOW LIGHT IS FLASHING. The yellow light was not flashing. Louise Keeley couldn't bring herself to look out the window. She huddled with Kevin in the backseat and tried to put a brave face on the situation.

"This is less like Palm Beach than I imagined," she said, attempting levity.

Barbara, mortified, pushed back her cuticles and tried to act blasé. "Oh, well, you know how it is," she said. "This was all sand when they bought here. This . . . . just . . . sort of grew up around them while they were in Greece." She shrugged. "What can you do?"

The senator shrugged back. "Gee, I don't know," he said sarcastically. "Move?"

Barbara blanched. "Well, sure. But that's letting *them* win." She jerked her thumb out the window.

"I could live with that," he said. "Couldn't you, Louise?"

She nodded. "I could live with that."

Behind them, in the silver Escort, Harry Radman was matching their progress, and his keen eye missed nothing of what was going on around them. Senator Kevin Keeley, cofounder of the Coalition for Moral Order, trolling the Babylonian main drag in South Beach, Florida. It was too good to be true. He pinched himself to see if he was dreaming.

The Escort came to a halt as a tall, lanky, sweaty black man with hoop earrings, dressed only in what looked like a hotel towel (*safety-pinned* at his hip, no less), ran desperately among the cars, crying, *"Where's my python? Has anyone seen my python?"* He cupped his hands and peered into the Keeleys' car. "Please, please— have you seen my python?"

Radman turned to Fishburn, grinning happily, and said, "Pal, we better clear shelf space for a couple of Pulitzers."

Chapter
thirty-one

armand and Val stood at the door to the bedroom. Armand tried the handle; the door wouldn't give.

He turned to Val and raised his eyebrows hopefully. "If we're lucky, he won't come out at all." He pivoted his head and addressed the looming crucifix. "I'm not religious. And I'm Jewish besides. But if everything goes all right tonight, I'll buy you."

The doorbell rang.

Val and Armand looked at each other, hearts pounding like pistons. "Amen," said Val.

"You said it, I didn't."

"And speaking of Jewish," Val said, as he and Armand turned to face the Keeleys, "Barbara told her parents our last name is Coleman."

Armand stopped short. *"What?"*

The doorbell rang again. Agador bolted into the foyer. He was wearing highly polished black shoes, and, as he'd warned Val, they caused him to trip and fall—and fall theatrically at that, arms flailing, legs dovetailing in the air.

the birdcage

Armand turned to the crucifix and dropped an acerbic, "Thanks."

Agador groaned, got to his feet, and opened the door.

A distinguished, red-faced man in a suit, a diminutive and nervous-looking middle-aged woman, and an enchanting gamine stood revealed; the Keeleys, of course. Who else?

Agador bowed deeply, and in his new Marlboro Man voice, said, "Good evening. I am Spartacus, the Goldmans' butler."

Armand threw another glance at the crucifix. "Perfect," he muttered. "Keep it up. Already met your quota of converts this month, have you? One more heathen just not worth the effort?"

Senator Keeley squinted and cocked his head. *"Goldman?"* he said.

Val rushed forward and said, "No, no, *Coleman.* Spartacus is—is—"

"Guatemalan," said Armand.

"—new," said Val. He ushered the Keeleys in.

Barbara kissed him (rather sisterly, he thought, on the cheek) and said, "Val, this is my father and mother." She turned to her parents. "This is Val Coleman."

Senator Keeley, who hadn't reached his station in life for nothing, fixed his eye on the boy and said, "Coleman? Or Coldman?"

Armand stepped forward and extended his hand. "Coleman," he said, smiling winningly. "The 'd' is silent."

Val gestured toward him. "My father."

Armand bowed and took Mrs. Keeley's hand in his. "How do you do."

Louise looked somewhat abashed, and made a girl-

143

ishly guilty face at her husband. "Oh," she said, gently withdrawing her hand. "My daughter, Barbara . . ." She moved Barbara bodily in front of her.

Armand renewed his bow and took Barbara's hand. "Delighted." He feigned a kiss over her knuckles. Barbara made a face at Val, as if to say, What is this?

Val rolled his eyes in reply.

Mrs. Keeley placed a hand on the senator's shoulder. "My husband."

"Extremely honored," said Armand fulsomely. He thrust his hand out from the shoulder, his wrist rigid. Senator Keeley blinked at this Frankenstein-like move, then held out his own hand. They shook, and as they did so, Senator Keeley winced at Armand's grip. He yanked his hand away, and laughed nervously. "You have a forceful handshake, Mr. Coleman," he said.

Armand nodded. "Well. You have to. In Greece."

There was a tiny pause, while everyone pretended to know what that meant.

Finally, Val broke the silence. "My mother won't be here for another ten or fifteen minutes," he said amiably. "She's . . . she's visiting my grandparents. In Palm Springs. And . . . and the traffic . . . you know."

"Oh, isn't that nice," said Mrs. Keeley, who was positively willing everything to be perfect. "To have such contact between the generations." She turned for confirmation to her husband, who was staring into the apartment, trying to make out its contours in the dim light.

"Yes," said Armand, to fill up the awkward pause that followed. "Um—won't you come in?"

He led them into the living room, walked slowly and stiffly, so as not to mince. The Keeleys followed, watching his tortured progress with some concern.

Val noticed this, and piped in with, "How's your leg,

Pop?" He turned to the Keeleys and said, "My father suffers from an old football injury."

"Ah!" said the senator, gratefully. "I thought I recognized a fellow sufferer. Where did you play?"

Val and Armand turned and looked at him with somewhat stricken faces; then Val said "Miami U." at the same time Armand blurted "Greece."

Before this could sink in, Barbara yanked her mother's arm and said, "What an interesting room! Oh, I love it. Look, Mother! Isn't this room nice?"

Mrs. Keeley looked at the room in question: to her taste, it seemed rather dark, and disconcertingly vacant. But she couldn't very well say so. "Um, yes," she said, thoughtfully. "Yes, very. A pleasant vacation house. I like its . . . its . . ." She fumbled for a word. ". . . severity."

Armand lowered his head in appreciation.

"Actually," said Val, stepping even farther into the room. "Pop uses this place more for work and, uh, reflection, than anything else. It's not so much a vacation house as a . . . a . . ."

"Monastery," said Armand, one eye on the traitorous crucifix.

"Yes, that," said Val, nodding enthusiastically.

"Well, it's just charming," said Mrs. Keeley, stepping well into it and placing her purse on the chair. "And what lovely old books!" She examined the spines of the volumes displayed on a credenza. *"Nancy Drew and the Case of the Burning Candle."* She smiled in surprise. "Why, you have the whole series!"

Val, momentarily confused, said, "What?—Oh. Yes. They're—my mother's."

"I loved them as a girl. We must compare notes! All my copies are gone, though." She sighed. "So much of childhood put aside! One wonders why, later in life . . ."

the birdcage

Her tone was turning faintly elegiac. Armand exchanged a worried look with Val, then turned to his guests.

"Please, please," he said. "Sit down."

They all found places on either the massively soft couch or the rigid Gothic chairs. Armand alone remained standing. "Shall we have some champagne to celebrate?" he said, ambling over to the bar.

"Oh, how nice!" said Mrs. Keeley, eagerly grabbing at another trivial nicety to support her view that everything was just perfect.

Armand craned his neck toward the corridor. "Agador!" he called out.

Val, to thwart disaster, immediately called out, "Spartacus!"

Armand, realizing his mistake, took a step forward and, even more loudly, called out, *"Agador Spartacus!"* Then he turned to the Keeleys and said, "He insists on being called by his full name."

Agador appeared in the doorway, his toes turned inward. "Yes, sir," he said, grimacing as if in pain.

"Bring in the champagne," Armand commanded him.

He limped out.

Armand took a seat next to Val, and the two of them sat smiling at the Keeleys. It was only then that Louise noted that both father and son were soaked with sweat.

Chapter
thirty-two

The silver Escort parked behind the black Lincoln. Only the chauffeur was left inside the latter.

"This is it," said Harry, unbuckling his seatbelt. "Wish me luck."

"Luck" said Fishburn, shifting into park.

Harry ambled up to the driver's window of the Lincoln and said, "Hey."

The driver hastily (and rather clumsily) closed up the skin magazine he'd been reading, and said, "Oh. Hello again."

"We followed you down here. Hope you don't mind."

"I expected as much." He stuffed the magazine under the seat. "And, of course, I spotted you en route."

Harry smiled and nodded. "You're good at this," he said, trying to stroke the chauffeur's ego with a little positive reinforcement. "Have to wake up early, to get one past you."

The chauffeur lifted his head smugly. "Well, there's more to me than meets the eye, you know."

Radman nodded at the building adjacent to them; a

nightclub, it looked like. Neon sign read THE BIRDCAGE. "They in here?" he asked hopefully.

The chauffeur shook his head. "They went around the corner," he said, jerking his head in that direction.

Harry tipped his hat, said "Thanks, buddy," and returned to the Escort. He leaned into the driver's window, and said, "Around the corner."

Fishburn craned his neck to see where Harry was pointing. "Yeah? . . . That's the side entrance to this building." He looked back at The Birdcage. "Wonder if it leads to the club."

"Let's check it out," said Harry, rubbing his hands together greedily.

Fishburn got out of the car, slammed shut the door, and pressed the alarm button on his key chain; the car gave a little eep of confirmation, flashed its lights, and was silent.

Harry shook his head. "As if anyone'd steal that pile of shit."

"Maybe it is, but it's *my* pile of shit." He hitched up his pants. "Didn't see you jumping up to volunteer *your* car for this job."

Harry reddened. "It's in the shop."

"It's in the shop," repeated Fishburn, who clearly didn't believe this. "All right, let's go."

Before they could step away from the car, a lanky, jumpsuited girl with wild, honey-colored hair approached them. "Excuse me!" she cried, in deep, throaty tones. "Excuse me, dears!"

Harry turned and was stunned at the sight of this apparition. "Uh—wha—yes?" he said, exchanging a quick glance with Fishburn.

The girl was directly in front of them now; close enough to reveal that she was no girl at all. "You don't mean to park here, do you?" she said. "Very, very not allowed! Our valet is off seeing to someone's car. He'll be back in, oh, just seconds!"

Harry stared at her with his mouth open. "Well—we'll—we'll just be—we'll just be a moment," he said, not daring to take his eyes off her. "A moment."

She grimaced. "Well. All right. But if you're here much longer, you'll probably be towed. Just so you're warned." She turned and clip-clopped back into the club.

Harry looked at Fishburn, then held up a finger to silence him. "Don't," he said. "Don't say a word." He shook his head. "You'll jinx it."

Fishburn made a zipping motion across his lips.

Chapter
thirty-three

S uch a responsibility," said Mrs. Keeley as she leaned forward and clasped her hands at her knees. "Two houses. How long ago did you buy this one?"

"About fifteen years ago," said Armand, mopping his brow. He lowered his voice and said, in deepest confidence, "Of course, the area then was mostly *Jewish*."

The senator nodded soberly.

But Mrs. Keeley looked at him curiously. "Really?" she said. "Barbara was telling us it was mostly sand."

"Yes. Well," said Armand, mopping his brow again. "You know the old saying, 'Where there's sand . . .'" He trailed off into silence, and raised his eyebrow.

Mrs. Keeley nodded knowingly, but found herself unable to respond.

Agador chose that exact moment to limp in with a bottle of champagne in a bucket. He seemed to be having even more difficulty walking than before; he looked as though he were crossing a rope bridge in a windstorm.

"Ah!" said Armand at the sight of him. "Here we go. Champagne for everyone."

"And a Scotch," interjected the senator. "If you have it."

"Scotch!" said Armand, uncertainly. "Why, I'm certain we—we probably—Agador Spartacus, a Scotch for the senator!" Having delegated the problem, he sat back and relaxed.

Agador set the bucket on the table between them, then took the bottle and started to twist off its cork. Everyone watched him in anticipation, and the small silence that accompanied this was at one point interrupted by a little *thunk* from another room.

The Keeleys turned. "Did you hear that?" the senator asked.

"Hear what?" Armand asked blankly.

"Is someone else home?" Mrs. Keeley inquired. "Should we put off our drinks?"

Armand laughed very loudly, and a trifle too long. "Just our dog, Piranha," he said merrily. "We lock her in when there's company."

The cork suddenly exploded across the room. Both Agador and Armand squealed in terror. Val covered up this gaffe by grabbing the bottle from the manservant with a yelp of glee.

"Thank you, Agador Spartacus," he said hastily. "I'll do the pouring. You take care of dinner."

Agador bowed sheepishly, then teetered out. Val made the rounds, filling the crystal flutes.

"He's a brilliant chef," said Armand of the departing Agador, "but he still has a lot to learn about serving."

Louise Keeley nodded in sympathy. "Good help—it's such a cliché, but it is true. So hard to find." She put her hand on her chin. "Does he have a palsy? He seems very uncertain on his feet."

"Oh, that," Armand said with a chuckle. "Recent surgery. He—he—had a vasectomy."

"A vasectomy?"

"Yes. Quite a man with the ladies, is Agador. Agador Spartacus. Had to have one, for his own financial well-being. Just went under the knife yesterday. Hasn't quite regained his sea legs."

"Oh, my word," said Mrs. Keeley, putting her hand to her throat. "Surely he ought to be on his back, recuperating!"

"Being on his back was what got him in trouble in the first place," joked Armand. They fell silent as Agador hobbled back in with the largest tumbler of Scotch the senator had ever seen. He handed it to him, then departed again.

Armand glanced nervously at his watch. "Where could my wife be?" he said with a little laugh.

By his wife, he of course meant Katharine, who at that moment was stuck in traffic before an open bridge in midtown. As car horns blared all around her, with complete and (she thought) contemptible futility, she grimaced in disgust and put her car in park, then opened her purse and took out several slips of paper.

Barbara and Val had meanwhile taken center stage, and were recounting the story of their courtship.

"He was—he was, like, so weird," said Barbara, pulling her hair behind her ears.

Val nodded, laughing although embarrassed. "I really was," he said, covering his forehead with his hand. "I was all, 'Will you marry me?' and she was all, 'Excuse me? But aren't you the guy who said, "No way before thirty"?' And I was all, 'Don't remind me.'" He and Barbara clutched their sides as they laughed; their parents nodded in good-natured, if confused, agreement.

"Oh, it was *so* funny," said Barbara, reaching for another sip of her champagne.

"Yes," said Mrs. Keeley with a broad, false smile. "It . . . it *does* sound funny."

Another *thunk*. The Keeleys' eyes darted toward the corridor.

Val jumped into the silence. "Did you have a good trip, senator?"

"What? Uh . . . yes. Yes. A good trip. Very nice." He crossed his legs. "We decided to drive here, to . . . to see the seasons change. It was a long trip—down through Virginia, Kentucky, Tennessee, Georgia—but it's just so magical to me . . ." The phone rang. Neither Val nor Armand made a move to answer it; both looked at Senator Keeley as though in thrall to his story. He decided he'd best continue. He cleared his throat, took another sip from his half-pint of Scotch, and said, "To come from the north where it's so cold, to the south . . ." Another ring. ". . . where it's so warm, and see the tremendous differences from region . . ." A third ring. ". . . to region in this incredible country of ours. My wife and I used to drive . . ." A fourth ring. ". . . down to Virginia every autumn, to see the foliage turn. Amazing foliage— although I think the foliage in Ohio is underrated. Just dazzling along I-75 . . ."

There was a sudden series of clicks, and then Katharine's voice came over the answering machine, loud and clear. Val and Armand remained motionless, sickly smiles plastered on their faces, their eyes riveted into their guests'. After a moment of uncertainty, the senator, sensing that he was expected to do so, went on.

"Hello? Hello?" Katharine said. "It's Katharine. Armand? Val? . . . Albert?"

"Just . . . dazzling along I-75. Um . . . but we'd drive to Virginia, just to get away . . ."

"Oh, shit. Listen, I'm stuck in traffic, can you start dinner without me?"

". . . you know, see the wonderful farms and the countryside. Just beautiful. You should see the hills . . ."

Val, never taking his eyes off the senator, or allowing his frozen smile to wilt, rose, backed up toward the answering machine, and silently, gracefully, shut it off.

". . . the hills," said the senator, now without any accompaniment. "Talk about purple mountains' majesty! Just fantastic. Red leaves, purple mountains, green fields—and the roads! Black. Just cutting through the green All the colors, the trees . . ." He paused and drew a deep breath, having nearly exhausted himself. He took another mouthful of Scotch, then turned back to his hosts. "Pennsylvania is nice, too," he said, charitably.

There followed another, longer pause. Then, as if having just thought of this, Armand turned to Val and said, "Was that your mother? Just now? On the phone? I think it was. I was just so caught up in . . ."

"Yes," said Val, nodding rapidly. "Yes, it was Mother. She's stuck in traffic and she wants us to start dinner without her." He turned to the Keeleys and said, "I should have picked up, but I didn't want to interrupt the senator's fascinating story."

Senator Keeley regarded him with reluctant pride. "Well, it wasn't *that* good . . ."

"It was wonderful!" said Armand. "I could almost imagine I was there! Such color and texture. You have a gift!" He clapped his hands and said, "Well, I'd better tell Agador Spartacus the news . . ."

He rose from his chair rather swishily, with his knees clasped together. Val leapt to his side. "Let me help you, Pop." He winked at the Keeleys, as if to remind them of the old football injury. "Will you excuse us?"

Val led him rather forcefully to the patio. Then, smil-

the birdcage

ing widely, he shut the glass door, then whirled on his father. "Pop!"

"I know, I know," said Armand softly. He leaned against the railing and put his hand on his heart. "I've never had so much go wrong so quickly. And I'm in the cabaret business!" He shook his head. "This is like a curse."

Val leaned against the wall next to the door. "What'll we do? Should we try and wait for her? Oh, God, this is *awful* . . ." He craned his neck into the doorframe and waved.

The Keeleys waved back with muted enthusiasm. Then, the senator leaned forward and whispered to his family. "Something odd is going on."

"It's this thing with Jackson," said Mrs. Keeley in a bit of a panic. "The wife probably doesn't want to be in the same house with us. Not that I can blame her! And the father's clearly a nervous wreck. We're pariahs, Kevin!"

"No, no," said Barbara. "I'm sure that's not it."

"But there's something else," said the senator as he rubbed his chin thoughtfully. "Something about the father . . . and the butler. I can't put my finger on it . . ."

"It's *nothing,*" said Barbara testily. "Why must you always think the worst? Val's mother is just a little late. That's all."

"Excuse me," said Armand. He'd stepped back in from the patio, and Val was behind him, running his fingers nervously through his hair. He looked absolutely ashen. Barbara wanted to die for him. "We'll . . . we'll give her half an hour." Armand continued. "And then if she isn't here, we'll—"

"Here I am!" rang a voice from the corridor beyond.

Albert's voice.

Armand and Val didn't dare turn yet; they were too busy inventing possible excuses, none of which was even

155

remotely believable. And when they at last faced front and gave Albert their full notice, they discovered him in a conservative skirt, short jacket, and white gloves, wearing one of his flamboyant wigs that had been trimmed and sprayed into such submission that it might have passed muster with the Daughters of the American Revolution. There was a little fur stole around his shoulders, and he carried an outsize purse.

Armand and Val stared at him, frozen with mortification.

"Please forgive me for being so late," he trilled as he approached. He smiled at Senator Keeley, who politely leapt to his feet. "Traffic was unbelievable! Senator Keeley, Mrs. Keeley—I'm so happy to meet you at last." He shook their hands, then turned to Barbara, whose jaw was hanging slack. "And you must be my daughter-in-law to be! What a pretty child. Come here and give me a hug." Barbara's eyes grew wide. "Don't be afraid!" Albert urged her. In response, she gripped the arms of her chair. "Oh, how adorable," said Albert, turning back to the Keeleys. "She's shy!"

Mrs. Keeley smiled happily. "It's so nice to meet you, Mrs. Coleman."

"Goldman," said Albert, correcting her with a wink.

Senator Keeley cocked his head. "I thought the 'd' was silent."

"What? The—"

"It *is* pronounced Coleman, isn't it?" said Barbara pointedly. "We've had some confusion."

"*Cole*man?" said Albert. He turned to Armand, who gave him a positively soul-shattering glare.

"Oh, *yes*," said Albert, catching on at last. "Coleman! The 'd' is silent in America." He waved a hand, as if this detail were one of many he had to work hard to keep straight. "It's Cole'd'isle au Man, or Cole of the Isle of

Man, in France, where Armand's chateau is, and Cole d'man in Greece, where Armand's work is, and finally, the vulgar Coleman here in Florida, where Armand's home is . . . so actually, we don't know where we are until we hear our last name pronounced." He laughed ringingly.

"Oh, *I* see," said Louise Keeley, who had missed most of the flurry of details, but not the gist. "Well, that explains it."

"Yes. At last," said the senator with satisfaction. He folded his hands behind his back and smiled contentedly.

Barbara, charmed by Albert's ingenuity, got up out of her chair and said, "I think I *would* like to hug you, Mrs. Coleman."

Chapter
thirty-four

It was getting to be another late night in the edit room. Not that those were unusual for Barney Pirskin. He'd had more than his fair share of grim microwaved dinners wolfed down just in time for Leno, and this week was no exception. Even his cat was beginning to look at him as though he were a trespasser in her house.

His producer stood over his shoulder and breathed down his neck—annoying habit. They were going over the rolls and rolls of footage shot the night before outside Senator Kevin Keeley's big old mansion in Ohio. Not a lot of action in them yet; the networks had already taken and aired the prime stuff, which included a hilarious interview with the senator while he was perched atop a ladder. Most of this stuff, by contrast, was just shots of the house and grounds—though occasionally the wife would walk by a window, all dolled up like she was going to a state dinner. But the producer was all hot to see it again, for some reason. He shuttled through it as quickly as he could.

"Okay," said the producer, eyeing the digital counter. "Slow down. It's around 2883."

Barney brought the tape back into real time, and sat back.

A reporter—slim, efficient, but fuckable—burst into the suite. "All right," she said, throwing her briefcase onto a chair. "Five minutes, then I'm heading home. You got something for me or not?"

"*You* be the judge," said the producer smugly. He stepped aside to let the reporter stand over Barney. He didn't mind *her* breath on his neck nearly as much.

The counter reached 2874; on-screen were grainy, random images of the mansion's grounds shot, Barney imagined, from a short distance away. Probably in the street.

"Here," said the producer, as the counter hit 2881.

The camera had settled on the driveway of the house, where, almost unnoticeably, a guy in a trench coat was reaching through the rails of the gate.

"We were going through footage for the special on Eli Jackson," said the producer. Just as he said this, someone—a chauffeur, Barney guessed by the uniform—appeared on-screen, crossing the driveway and approaching the guy in the trench coat. "Can you pump up the sound?" the producer asked.

Barney flipped the audio to full. Through the hiss and crackle of the tape, they could pretty clearly hear the trench-coated guy ask, "Where are you driving him?"—followed by the chauffeur replying, "South Beach, Florida. Tonight."

The reporter stood up and pursed her lips, clearly impressed.

"Thanks, Barney," the producer said, with a condescending pat on the shoulder. Barney froze the tape on a frame of the chauffeur taking money from Mr. Trench Coat, and swiveled his chair around so he could stretch his legs.

"Where'd we get this?" the reporter asked briskly.

"Keeley's house last night. Shooting cutaways. The fat guy is with the *Enquirer*. Harry . . . Harry Radman," he said, checking his notepad.

The reporter said, "Radman?" and leaned in to look at the screen again. "My God, he's really put on weight since the Simpson case." She stood up again. "Maybe this should go to the network."

Barney smiled as the reporter and producer exited, deep in conversation, having completely forgotten him. It looked like it might be an earlier night than he'd expected.

Chapter
thirty-five

arry Radman could feel it—the deepening sense of focus and calm he experienced whenever he was close to his prey. He imagined that the lions and leopards he'd seen in wildlife TV shows felt the same way when, after having crept and crawled agonizingly slowly through the short, dry grasses, they were close enough to hurl themselves at a stunned antelope, knowing there was no chance of it escaping. It was all over but the kill, now. Especially since the chauffeur, ever eager to be of help, had given them a name for another measly fifty. He was on his cellular phone now, checking it out with the *Enquirer*'s computer nerve center in New York.

He peered at the card above the doorbell and spoke into a cellular phone. "C-o-l-e-m-a-n," he said, scanning the card. "No, it's not on the bell. Sorry. But . . . yeah, I'll hold." He stood at the side of the building, trying to be inconspicuous, while the name was checked out. But it was hard to be inconspicuous when you were with a six-foot-four photographer with bright red hair. "You're sure?" He turned to Fishburn. "No Coleman listed here."

"Maybe it's the wrong address."

Harry scowled. "I thought of that. But the chauffeur swears he dropped them off here. Saw them go round the corner. The corner that leads right to this door."

"Maybe they were tryin' to fool him. Throw him off the scent."

Harry made a face. This guy might be a good photographer, but he had the journalistic instincts of a parakeet. "Why would they do that? The guy *works* for them."

"Maybe they suspect that he's informin' the media."

"He's not informing the media, he's only informing me. And if they suspected him of that, he wouldn't have made it this far." Then, his irritation vented, he let his shoulders slump and—awful sensation—started feeling some of his focus and calm slip away. As though, at the last moment, the antelope had sprouted wings and flown out of his grasp.

"All right," he said at last, "it's not likely, but we'll try it." He spoke into the phone again. "Listen, try the surrounding addresses. Look for a Coleman anywhere in the zip code, for God's sake. In fact, just give me anything you've got on any Coleman anywhere in South Beach. There's gotta be a connection here, somewhere." He paused. "Yeah, I know it'll take some time. I'll hold."

They waited. A red-faced, burly man in a bloody apron came out of the building next door, scowled at them, then took a foul-smelling bag to the back of the building.

Fishburn wrinkled his forehead and said, "Hey. What about the name we saw on the door of that club up front? Goldman. Coleman and Goldman are pretty damned close."

Harry's eyes twinkled wickedly. In his head, he apologized for having disdained this kid's instincts. "You're right," he said. "Wouldn't that be something?" He lifted the phone to his jaw again and said, "Hello? Hello? You there? Stop the search—I got something else I want you to try . . ."

Chapter
thirty-six

---

the Keeleys and the "Colemans," much more relaxed with each other now, were all seated around a spare coffee table, chatting. They'd killed off the champagne and had moved on to mixed drinks. Senator Keeley was still working his way through his mammoth Scotch.

"It's just wonderful what you've done here," Mrs. Keeley enthused. "Everything so simple and uncluttered. Our place is just a sea of papers." She teasingly shook her finger at her husband. "You men! You're the biggest babies." She turned back to Albert and winked. "They can run the world, but they can't choose a tie."

Albert squeezed her forearm in sympathy. "I know. I can't get this big lug to buy a new suit."

Senator Keeley chuckled, then said, "Armand, they're picking on us!"

Armand, still unable to quell his outrage over Albert's stunt, simply said, "Yes."

"Well, bless them," Albert said, beaming maternally on Armand and the senator. "That's the way nature made them. Maybe I'm just an old-fashioned girl, but I pity the woman who's too busy to stay home and take care of her man.''

Barbara stiffened, but Senator Keeley raised his glass. ''Hear, hear!'' he said genially. ''God, it's *so* nice to meet people like you.''

Albert smiled beatifically at the compliment. ''Well, Armand and I feel likewise. There are so few standards left, these days. It feels . . . well, almost *vindicating* to actually meet fellow standard-bearers.''

The senator turned to his wife. ''Did you hear that, Louise? 'Fellow standard-bearers.' By God, I like that! Do you mind if I steal that from you, Mrs. Coleman?''

''Oh, gracious, no. Anything that will aid you in your crusade, Senator Keeley. Heavens, with all the social ills plaguing our society today, from sex education in schools to eliminating school prayer, I'd be a criminal not to allow you any weapon you might need for your arsenal! Although I'm very flattered you think enough of my little phrase to want it all. Are you proud of your mother, dear?'' He turned to Val and eyed him inquiringly; Val, for his part, stared back in dumbfounded fear.

The senator was nodding madly. ''Oh, you good woman. I *do* need help, believe me, and thank you sincerely for it. If you only knew the perniciousness of our foes—! It beggars description. And certainly defies logic! Take this fuss over school prayer. As if anyone—Jews, Moslems, whatever—would *mind* if their children prayed in the classroom.''

''Daddy,'' said Barbara tentatively. She sensed Val approaching a nervous collapse.

''It's insane,'' said Albert fiercely, rapping on the arm of his chair.

Agador chose this opportune moment to enter with a bucket of ice. He carried it soberly, his tongue curled

the birdcage

around one cheek, until he saw Albert; then he burst into wild, hyena-like laughter.

"Thank you, Agador Spartacus," said Armand tersely. "You may go."

Agador recognized the deathly fury in his master's voice, so he set the bucket down and shuffled away, giggling.

The Keeleys stared after him, astonished by his outburst. Albert leaned forward and, in a stage whisper, said, "He's very nice, but he's such a problem! We never know what makes him laugh."

Mrs. Keeley nodded. "At least he speaks English. If you *knew* how many chauffeurs we've run through in the last six months . . ."

"Latest fellow seems all right," said the senator. "Speaks English perfectly. But then, he's perfectly American." He puts his finger on the side of his nose. "And there you have it."

"If you knew how many *maids* we've run through in the last six years," Albert said with a sigh. "I could name a dozen: Rodney, Julian, Bruce . . ."

"Oh, look!" said Armand, interrupting him before he got too far with this. They've all turned his way, perplexed.

He broke out into a fresh sweat. "You—you all need more ice in your drinks!" He jumped out of his chair, picked up the ice bucket and tongs, and made his way around the room, dropping ice into their various glasses.

"You know," said the senator, "I really have such a good feeling about you people. Not a lot of 'clever' books on the shelves, not a lot of fancy 'art' on the walls—just the crucifix and a lot of good, warm, family being. *This* is what Clinton didn't understand when he started in on school prayer and gays in the military . . ."

"And more ice for you," said Armand, deliberately

dropping the ice from such a height that it splashed Scotch onto the senator's pants.

"Now *there's* an idiotic issue," said Albert, as the senator mopped his thigh with a napkin. "Gays in the military. I mean, those haircuts, those uniforms—who cares?" He shook his head and laughed softly; but when he turned for a corroboratory glance from Mrs. Keeley, he found her staring at him with increasing bafflement.

"Now, Mom," said Val, a bead of sweat under each earlobe, "you shouldn't be talking about things you *don't know about.*" He bit off each of the words. "Please . . ."

Senator Keeley shook his finger at him. "Val, don't you patronize your mother. She's an amazingly intelligent woman. I think homosexuality . . ."

"And a *lot* more ice for you," said Armand, plunking in a few more cubes and blocking the senator from the others.

But he was not to be deterred; he spoke around Armand. ". . . is one of the things that's weakening this country."

"You know," said Albert, "that's what *I* thought until I found out Alexander the Great was a fag. Talk about gays in the military!"

"How about those Dolphins!" bellowed Armand.

They all looked at him mutely. Not knowing what else to do, he dropped the ice bucket.

Val leapt to his feet. "Oh! I'll get it."

As he and Armand scrambled to pick up the spilled ice, Senator Keeley took a deep breath, then put his drink down and said, "Look, I think . . . I think we've been skirting an issue that has Mr. Coleman very nervous. And I don't blame him."

Val and Armand ceased their cleanup and looked at him with wide, fearful eyes; so did Albert.

He cleared his throat and continued. "I know you've

heard the terrible news about Senator Jackson . . . how he died . . .''

Albert nearly fainted from relief. "Oh, *that*. Yes. What an ugly story. Of course, we don't believe a word of it."

"What—what do you mean, Mrs. Coleman?"

"He was obviously framed. And I, for one, would like an autopsy."

Val got to his feet. "Uh . . . *Mom* . . ."

The senator was shaking his head in wonder. "That's just what Rush Limbaugh said!"

Armand got to his feet as well. He smiled with as much sincerity as he could, then said, "Excuse me," and hurried out of the room.

He staggered into the kitchen, fell into a chair, and put his head between his knees. Agador, not the least bit surprised by his appearance, poured a drink and handed it to him. He tossed it back and gasped.

"I've never felt such tension," he said, half to Agador, half to himself. "It's like riding a psychotic horse toward a burning stable."

Agador, however, was deep within a crisis of his own. The counter was spread with foodstuffs, and there were pots and pans in profusion, but when he looked at it, all he could see was chaos. What to put where? And when? And for how long? He'd never dreamed it could be so confusing.

"Dinner will be late," he said dreamily. "I . . . I had so little time to shop . . ."

"But the girl's nice," said Armand, taking the bottle from where Agador had set it, and downing a large swig right from the source. "And I owe it to Val. Growing up the way he did . . . it can't have been easy . . ."

"And I'm *really* sorry about laughing at Miss Albert," Agador continued, as he chopped at a floret of broccoli until it was almost completely atomized. "It was just—that *hairdo*."

"Fuck it," said Armand, slamming the bottle back on the counter "It's one night. I can live through it." He stood up, puffed out his chest, and strode manfully out of the kitchen.

He arrived back at the living room just in time to hear Senator Keeley concede, ". . . of course, it's very wrong to kill an abortion doctor . . ."

Armand clutched his heart and his step faltered.

Val leapt up. "Pop?"

Weakly, he said, "I'm here, son," and made his way to his chair. He dropped into it like a wrecking ball.

"But, you know," continued the senator, speaking almost directly to Albert now, "so many pro-lifers—and I can't stress enough that I don't agree with them—sincerely believe that stopping the doctors will stop the abortions."

"Well, that's just ridiculous," said Albert, downing the last of his drink. "The doctors are just doing their jobs." He set the glass on the table, then leaned forward and said, "If you're going to kill someone, kill the mothers. *That*'ll stop 'em."

Louise Keeley let out a little hiccup of alarm. A moment of stunned silence enveloped them all.

"Dear," said Armand through a clenched-teeth smile, "may I see you for a second?"

"I know what you're going to say," Albert continued, ignoring Armand. "If you kill the mother, the fetus dies too. But the fetus is going to be aborted anyway, so why not let it go down with the ship?"

Armand put some iron into his voice. "I really *must* see you. *Now*."

Albert crinkled his nose at the senator. "Excuse me,"

he said coquettishly. He rose from the chair, smoothed his dress, and followed Armand out of the room.

A deathly silence settled on those remaining. Barbara threw desperate glances at Val, begging him to say something.

Finally, Val swallowed hard and said, "I assure you that my . . . my mother is just following out a train of thought to its logical and absurd conclusion. Very much the way Jonathan Swift did when he suggested the Irish peasants feed their babies to the rich."

Senator Keeley raised his eyebrows. "Well, I don't know anything about Jonathan Swift. But I know one thing about your mother—she's a passionate woman who follows her heart. And I just love her." He smiled with more sincerity and warmth than Val had ever dreamed he could possess.

Val and Barbara exchanged another glance, not knowing whether this development was a triumph or a disaster.

Chapter
thirty-seven

---

harry Radman was on the phone with the *Enquirer* nerve center.

"So, in other words, Goldman owns the club, *and* lives above it, *and* owns the building . . . *and* he's gay." He turned to Fishburn. "We're in *Enquirer* heaven."

"That's the gist of it," said Floyd, his contact. "I can also tell you his annual income, long-distance service, and five favorite catalogs, if you want. God, I love the twentieth century!"

"Thanks," said Radman. "Call you back if I need any of that."

"I don't know what you and the Fish are gonna do now," said Floyd. "But I'd do it quick. Story this big, it ain't gonna stay a secret for long."

And sure enough, at that very moment in a large network newsroom, just off to the side of an enormous, open set, a frosty-haired and self-important Executive Producer was seated at a bank of telephones, cradling the phone with his shoulder while he popped cough drops with one hand and took notes with the other. Next to him, an editor, a nervous-looking, prematurely balding man in glasses, stood trying to wait patiently.

". . . black Lincoln," the Executive Producer said, scrawling furiously. "Ohio plates . . . Got it." He paused for another cough drop. "Well, it's a small area. If he's there, they'll spot him."

He hung up, then turned and offered the editor a lozenge.

The editor declined by politely shaking his head, but was clearly ready to explode with curiosity. He'd been at the network for nine months without ever having worked on a breaking story, and the shame of it had begun to tie knots in his stomach.

"Kevin Keeley slipped off to South Beach," said the Executive Producer, sucking on the cough drop. "And the *National Enquirer* is tracking him." He ripped the sheet with his notes from the top of the pad, and handed it to the editor. "Call Miami and tell them to get on it. This could be real news."

By the time the editor had flown gleefully out of the newsroom, Harry Radman had set up a Birdcage-side vigil with Fishburn.

Chapter
thirty-eight

$a$rmand was at the piano, playing "I Could Have Danced All Night" with great flourish. Albert was dancing with Senator Keeley, and singing the lyrics into his ear; the senator looked blissfully happy.

Val was dancing with Barbara, and despite the house-of-cards character of the evening, they were actually enjoying themselves.

Mrs. Keeley sat on the piano bench and sang along, though her knowledge of the words wasn't quite as sure as Albert's.

Barbara leaned into Val and said, "I hope your mother knows I'm going to have a career after we're married."

"Barbara, Albert is not my mother. He's a drag queen."

Barbara blushed and buried her face in his shoulder for a moment. "That's right. My God. I can't . . ." She giggled. One drink too many, thought Val. "He just *sounds* so much like a mother."

They arrived at the last line of the song. At this climactic moment, Agador stepped into the doorway and, flinging his arms open, sang with them. "I could have danced, danced, *daaaanced* . . . all *niiiight!*"

They burst into genuine applause.

"What a lovely voice you have, Agador Spartacus!" said Mrs. Keeley, beaming at him appreciatively.

Agador bristled and threw a bitter glance at Armand. "*Thank* you, ma'am." Then he loftily addressed the gathering, sounding like a Third-World Arthur Treacher. "Dinner is served."

Senator Keeley offered Albert his arm. Barbara and Mrs. Keeley followed. Val hung back and looked at Armand questioningly.

Armand gestured for him to accompany the others. "Go on in," he said softly. "I'm going to write a note to Katharine and tape it to the door. Go on."

Reluctantly, Val complied.

When he reached the dining room, the guests were standing at the table, admiring the fresh flowers. Val looked back and saw Armand rushing around, apparently looking for a piece of paper to write on.

"Now, Mrs. Keeley, let's have you there," said Albert, pointing to a chair. "And the senator on my left. Val over there . . . Barbara there . . . please, everyone, sit."

Senator Keeley held out his chair for him. "Mrs. Coleman, you are the *most* gracious hostess."

He sat, and patted the senator's hand. "Thank you. Oh, I'm having such a *wonderful* time . . ."

In the living room, Armand had at last found a pad, and tore a sheet from it. As he wrote on it, he could hear Albert jabbering gaily through the open dining-room door.

"This is just what I've always dreamed of, a big, loving family . . ."

Katharine, he wrote at the top of the sheet.

". . . gathered around the table . . . just the way it was when I was a girl . . ."

He looked up, incredulous, then continued writing. *Plans have changed . . .*

"Yes," the senator said, "that's how we grew up, too."

"Oh, it was a wonderful world then, wasn't it?" Albert cooed.

Whatever you do, don't come upstairs.

"Happy families, and everyone speaking English, and no drugs and no AIDS . . ."

"Easy on the wine, Mom," said Val, an edge to his voice.

I'll call you tomorrow.

"What an interesting china," said Mrs. Keeley. "It looks like young men playing together. Is it Greek?"

Armand froze.

"I . . . I have no idea," said Albert. "I've never seen these bowls before."

"Really? Barbara, get my glasses, will you, dear? They're in my purse on the sofa."

He quickly wrote, *A million apologies, Armand,* and bolted toward the kitchen, nearly colliding with Barbara, who was on her way to fetch the purse.

In the meantime, Mrs. Keeley had picked up her soup bowl and was squinting into it. The senator was searching through his pockets. "Where are *my* glasses?" he said. Not finding them, he lifted the bowl and peered at it himself. "It *is* Greek . . . Greek boys, actually. Naked Greek boys . . ."

"And girls," said Albert with gentle insistence. "Don't you have any girls on your bowl?"

"*I* have one," piped Val.

"So do I," said Albert. "Look, Senator Keeley. There. I think that's a girl."

He looked to where Albert was pointing. "Then it's been a long time since you've seen one. Mrs. Coleman," he said, teasingly. "That's a boy. I may need glasses, but I can still see that."

Barbara darted in, clutching her mother's purse. "I couldn't find your glasses," she said, sneaking in a conspiratorial wink at Val. "Maybe you left them in the car."

"I must have mine somewhere," the senator muttered, rummaging through his jacket once more.

At this moment, Armand was in the kitchen, holding the handles to a large tureen while Agador ladled soup into it. He did so slowly and with excessive care, and paused once to drop in a few shrimp.

"Hurry, you idiot!" Armand barked. "They're sitting there looking at the bowls right now! What kind of moron sets the table without looking at the bowls?" Agador hissed at him and kept up his deliberate pace. "All right, stop ladling," said Armand, setting down the tureen. "Just give me the pot!"

Back in the dining room, Senator Keeley had stood up, and was checking his pants pockets. "It just drives me so damned crazy tha— wait. Here they are." He grinned triumphantly, produced his glasses, and put them on. "Now let's have a look at what those Greeks are doing."

He sat down and leaned over the bowl just as Armand appeared and ladled the soup into it.

"Here we go!" said Armand merrily. "We're in luck! Some of Agador's superb soup." He danced around the table to Mrs. Keeley's place. "Hmm. And it's his specialty." He ladled it lovingly into the bowl. "Seafood chowder."

Mrs. Keeley placed her hand on her breast and stared at the soup with some alarm. "Isn't . . . isn't that a hard-boiled egg?"

"What?" Armand looked into the bowl and suffered a momentary tic. Then he recovered and said, "Why, yes . . . it *is*! That's very . . . Guatemalan, you know. They put hard-boiled eggs in *everything* down there." He made his way around the rest of the table, lading as he spoke. "See, chicken is so important to them. It's their only real currency. A woman is said to be worth her weight in hens. A man's wealth is measured by the size of his cock." Val suffered a small coughing fit at this, so Armand stood back and quickly said, "Do you all have soup? Yes. Would you excuse me, then?"

He stormed back into the kitchen and thrust the pot under Agador's face. "What the hell are you serving us?"

Agador cringed in fright. "Sweet-and-sour peasant soup. I don't know why you called it seafood chowder."

Armand grimaced. "What's sweet-and-sour peasant soup?"

"I don't know! I made it up!"

Armand put down the pot and had another swig from the bottle. "My God! This is a nightmare!"

Faced with the strange soup, and with Armand's rather abrupt departure, the assembled guests had begun dining in a new, slightly awkward silence. Val occasionally grinned desperately at the Keeleys, and kept glancing toward the kitchen. Every so often, he checked his watch.

Albert broke the silence. "Where are you staying while you're in Florida?"

Mrs. Keeley pounced on the question, glad to be able to drop a name. "With the Bushes on Fisher Island. The *Jeb* Bushes."

"Oh, Fisher Island!" he trilled. "Such a lovely spot. My parents lived on Fisher Island till they died."

Val shook his head violently until Mrs. Keeley looked his way; then he elegantly segued into an equally vigorous nod.

The senator knit his brow. "Weren't you just visiting your parents in Palm Beach?"

"What?" said Albert, suddenly aware that he'd done it again. Armand and Val really might have shared with him a *little* of the backstory they'd prepared for Katharine. Didn't they *trust* him? He daubed his lips with a napkin and said, "Well, yes. Now. That they're dead. They've moved. *Were* moved. Because . . ." He smiled winningly and rested his hand on his chin. ". . . my mother always said, 'Live on Fisher Island, get buried in Palm Beach, that way you'll have the best of Florida."

Before anyone could think about this too deeply, Val jumped up and said, "Excuse me." Not allowing Barbara to catch his eye, he rushed out to the kitchen.

He found Agador weeping inconsolably in a corner. Armand was standing near the stove with his forehead pressed against the wall. "Pop!" he said. "You've got to get back in there! Everything's going to *hell*, Albert's about two breaths away from blowing everythi—"

He broke off as Armand spun his head and glared at him with crazy, wild eyes. "He didn't make an entrée," he said in a strangely flat voice.

Val's mouth fell open. "What do you mean? You mean . . . we just have *soup*?"

Agador took his hands from his face and sobbed, "P-p-peasant soup *is* an entrée. It's like a stew. That's why I put so m-much *into* it . . ."

Armand whirled on him. "Shut up!" He turned back to Val and thrust a piece of paper into the boy's hands. "Here. It's the note for Katharine. Put it on the outside door. I have to get back before they eat enough to see the bottom of the bowls."

"I had an *hour* to shop," wailed Agador, "a *million* things to do . . ."

"Shut *up*," Armand snarled at him again. Agador

curled up into the fetal position and started rocking, and Armand suddenly felt like a heel. ''All right, all right,'' he said in exhausted but conciliatory tones, ''stop crying, it's done.'' Then, under his breath. ''God*damn* you.'' He suddenly caught sight of Val, still standing there. ''Why are you still here? *Go!* She'll be here any minute.''

Val jumped to attention, suddenly realizing how events were bearing down on him. He snuck past the dining room to the front door, then raced down the stairs, murmuring prayers as he went.

Chapter
thirty-nine

m ere blocks away, a white van bearing the letters WXLT on its side moved slowly down the street. At the wheel was a young TV editor, Oscar, chewing madly on a wad of gum, and his pretty blond assistant, Faye, who wore an Alice in Chains T-shirt and held a slip of paper on her lap, looking utterly bored. She was twenty-one years old, it was a fabulous, warm night in South Beach, parties everywhere, and she was stuck in a news van with a geek ten years her senior, who chewed gum with his mouth open and talked nothing but politics.

Suddenly, Oscar straightened in his seat. "Up ahead," he said. "See if the black Lincoln has Ohio plates."

"Where?" Faye asked as she roused herself from her funk.

"There. Under the big neon sign on the club. The one with the chauffeur leaning against it."

She squinted at it, then at the paper. The numbers matched. "That's it. Pull over."

Oscar maneuvered the van into the only parking space on the street—in between a silver Escort and the black Lincoln—just as a dark-green BMW pulled a U-turn to get the same space.

Oscar stuck his head out the window and said, "Sorry."

The woman inside gave him a curse he could clearly lip-read, and sped off. Must be in a hurry, he thought. Not a bad looker, either: late thirties or early forties, but lean and fit. He wouldn't have minded a more complete view of her. Ah, well . . .

Unaware of the arrival of a competitor, Harry Radman was still by the side door of the building, waiting patiently for the next outbreak of action. Which, as it happened, had arrived. Just as he was about to risk another foray to the front of the building to see if any other media had caught the scent, the door opened, and a young man with longish hair, dressed in a dark suit, stepped out and looked from side to side. Harry and Fishburn ducked deeper into the shadows; the boy's eyes apparently didn't adjust to the darkness quickly enough to reveal them. He then turned, stuck a note to the front door, and darted back in.

They waited a few seconds just to be safe, then crept to the door; Harry grabbed the note and read it aloud.

" 'Katharine—Plans have changed. Whatever you do, don't come upstairs. I'll call you tomorrow. A million apologies, Armand.' " He shook his head, not believing his good fortune. "Fish, I don't know what it all means," he said, "but I do know it's going to be *great*."

Chapter
forty

———

The dinner guests had nearly finished with the soup. Val's chair was still empty, and the Keeleys' eyes kept darting toward it, then glancing at each other.

Albert, however, was wrapped up in the increasingly more baroque history of his parents. ". . . and from that day on," he said, nearly shedding a tear in spite of himself, "they decided to look for a cemetery they really loved instead of eating tofu. Daddy favored Key Biscayne, but Mummy was afraid of developers . . ."

Armand, keeping an eye on the Keeleys' bowls, leapt up as he caught sight of a Greek leg at the bottom of the senator's. "Another helping?" he said, wielding the tureen at him.

"Oh, no, no," said the senator, patting his belly.

Armand cheerfully ignored him and ladled in another bowlful.

Senator Keeley puffed his cheeks in irritation, then regained his composure and said, "Thank you. No more after this. I don't want to get too full."

"No fear of that," Armand mumbled bitterly. "Mrs. Keeley?"

Louise put her hands over her bowl as Armand approached. "No, really. I'm saving myself for the main course."

Armand hovered over her, ladle in midair, looking terribly guilty. "Oh! But I thought you understood . . ." He lowered the ladle and, in a daring move, began tilting it. Mrs. Keeley whipped her hands out of the way just as the soup cascaded into her bowl. ". . . this *is* the main course. In the Guatemalan jungle, peasant soup represents the coming-together, or pot-au-feu—everything in one pot." He drew himself up again and smiled. "Actually, every*one* in the pot, as they say in Agador's little village on bath night." He roared with laughter, oblivious to the uneasy faces of his guests.

"But, seriously," he continued, "when two families are about to unite, they dine together on peasant soup for the first meal—to symbolize that they're both going to be in the same . . ."

"Pot," interjected Albert merrily.

Armand glared at him. "Yes. Exactly."

Barbara pretended to be fascinated by this. "That's just so—incredible. Don't you think that's incredible, Dad?"

Senator Keeley was staring rather glumly at his new helping of soup. "I suppose."

"And this is such a great dish! Don't you think so, Mom?"

"Yes," said Mrs. Keeley, politely having another spoonful. "What . . . what gives the soup greens that . . . rather sweetish taste?"

Senator Keeley, who had taken another sip himself, chewed thoughtfully for a moment, then said, "Pineapple."

Val suddenly sprinted in, and, breathless, collapsed into his chair again. He smiled handsomely at everyone.

"There's Val," said Armand, setting the tureen on a serving table. "Just in time for dessert! Did you get everything done, son?"

"Yes, Pop."

Albert got to his feet. "Then shall we have our coffee in the living room?"

The Keeleys were caught in mid-mouthful by this unexpected end to the meal and were thus unable to object. They put down their spoons and obediently got to their feet.

Chapter
forty-one

Katharine had, through sheer determination, managed to wedge her BMW into a space any rational person would have said was far too small for it. She got out of the car and examined her handiwork. Each bumper was nearly touching the car facing it. She sighed, then looked at her watch and started running.

"Dammit, dammit, dammit," she said as she ran. It was a dark street, she was a woman with an expensive watch and a purse full of credit cards, and she was running; she might as well be wearing a Day-Glo banner that said VICTIM. And on top of that, she was exhausted from having fought the traffic all the way from Miami, right up to Armand's front door, where that fucking news truck had taken the space she'd coveted.

But as she approached the club, and the music grew louder, she found herself growing more energetic and excited. Seeing Armand again, after this afternoon. Seeing little Val again, after . . . well, twenty years, basically. What could be pleasanter? Nothing could spoil this night for her, nothing.

She rounded the corner and slowed to a brisk walk.

The lights were on her now, the crowd enveloped her. As she approached The Birdcage, she felt a twinge of envy at the little throng of decadent-looking persons filing under the neon sign and into the club. She'd never been daring enough to go; and after her heartbreak over Armand, she'd vowed never to try. She'd closed that door, good and hard.

Before she could feel any real chagrin, she spotted the driver of the news van—she'd never forget his sallow, taunting face—standing on the curb and jabbering excitedly into a cellular phone. She sneered at him; he didn't even notice her. A few steps beyond that, she saw a big black Lincoln parked just outside the club, with a liveried chauffeur leaning against its door. A luscious young blond in an Alice in Chains T-shirt was counting out bills and handing them to the chauffeur.

That's odd, she thought as she turned and headed for the side of the building. Every time she'd seen a transaction like that before, it had been the other way around.

Chapter
forty-two

---

gador had served the coffee without mishap—something of a miracle, given his hobbled gait and the teetering cups—and the evening was drawing to a close. The Keeleys and the "Colemans" were seated in the living room, sipping politely and eating bits of the cake that had once read *To my piglet, from his uncle,* but which now bore an extra layer of concealing frosting.

Barbara looked haggard. Val was dazed. Armand's suit was crumpled, his collar crushed, his tie hanging out. Albert's lipstick had melted. But they were still working. Maybe it was the momentum carrying them through: maybe it was the relative innocence of the Keeleys; maybe it was just sheer luck. However it happened, they were definitely still working.

"So," said Armand, just to fill up the silence till the Keeleys put down their cups and could be ushered out. "What do you think about these kids getting married?"

"Well," said the senator, "of course . . . she's not even eighteen, and he's only twenty, and so naturally we're concer—"

A blast of music from under their feet interrupted

186

him; he nearly spilled what was left of his coffee. Mrs. Keeley put down her saucer and put her hand on her breast and said," Oh, *my*."

"Good God," said the senator, "that sounds like it's coming from downstairs."

Louise cocked an ear. "It is! It must be from the nightclub on the corner. This," she said, suddenly realizing it, "this must be the same building!"

"You're joking!" said Albert, pretending shock. "I always thought that was someone's television set."

Armand reined him back in; he chuckled and said, "Now, darling—you *know* we live above a nightclub." He gave the Keeleys a commiserating look. "My wife has traveled all over the world with me, but deep down she's still the same little girl from Grovers Corners."

Relishing this role, Albert lowered his head and cooed, "Yes, I'm afraid I am a *bit* naive."

Senator Keeley leaned forward and said, with surprising fierceness, "Don't you be ashamed of Grovers Corners, Mrs. Coleman! It may not be a chateau in France, but it's a damned good place to call home."

The others regarded him with surprise; they were taken aback by his sudden intensity. The music was now quite loud, and there was a slight vibration; they could feel it in their teeth. Mrs. Keeley's cup was actually skittering slowly across the coffee table toward the edge, and she had to continually move it to the left. The whole scene began to take on an air of surreality.

Albert patted the senator's hand. "Oh, thank you, Kevin. May I call you Kevin? I *will* remember that. Of course, Armand is much more sophisticated than I am, but he comes from good stock . . ." He nodded, and without warning his wig slipped a good inch; not realizing this, he continued. ". . . and so do these two youngsters . . ."

Barbara saw the condition of the wig and jumped up in front of Albert.

"Where's the bathroom?" she said with some urgency.

Val got to his feet. "I'll show you."

"No. I want . . . I want Mother Coleman to show me."

Albert rose, his hand over his heart, an expression of luminous joy on his face. "Oh, my dear child . . ." Tears filled his eyes.

Armand suddenly caught sight of Albert's crooked wig and leapt up, too. He grasped Albert's head in his hands, trying to straighten it. "One kiss before you go," he said.

Albert pushed him away, astonished. "Dear, I'm only going to the bathroom."

The wig was now slightly worse. Val moved to the other side of Albert and said, "We'll all go. That's a pretty tough door to handle since the paint job."

"Well, I think you're all crazy," Albert said. He shook his head and the wig wobbled. "My men!" he said grandly, to the Keeleys.

Then he turned and started toward the bathroom, flanked by Armand and Val, their arms around his waist. Barbara rested her cheek against Albert's as they went, covering him from the front.

"This is so wonderful," Barbara said. "All of us together, all of us pot-au-feu."

Albert, deeply moved, felt his heart well up. "Oh, I think I'm going to cry. Oh, my goodness . . . I'm so happy." He began to weep as they walked him out of the room. The Keeleys sat staring after them, completely thunderstruck.

When they had gone, Louise leaned toward her husband and said, "Something *very* strange is going on here."

"I know," said the senator.

"That dinner! And I *know* there was something on those bowls. And the son disappearing like that while we were eating . . ."

"I know *just* what's going on."

She moved the cup and saucer from the brink yet again. "You do?"

"Of course I do," he said, nodding sagely. "It's the oldest story in the world."

"What is it?"

He crossed his legs. "She's a small-town girl and he's a pretentious European—the worst kind—with his Cole d' whatever and his decadent china. Oh, I've seen this before. Onassis was like this, and *all* the French, especially Mitterand, and the English—not Margaret Thatcher, of course, but you can't tell me John Major doesn't have something on the side and she just can't handle it."

"Who?"

"Mrs. Coleman."

"Why should she care about John Major?" She was growing more and more confused.

"No, no," said the senator, leaning forward again. "Mrs. Coleman can't handle *her* marriage to *him*—to Coleman, with his nasty little European traditions, and his snobbery, and that dig about Grovers Corners . . ."

She pushed the coffee cup away from the edge again. "Kevin, you're rambling."

"Well, I can't help it, it makes me furious to see the contempt he has for her. Did you see him while she was talking? He looked . . . almost *frightened*. And the son is patronizing, too. And that fake European courtliness—'One kiss before you go,' and the way he bowed when he was being introduced to you. Exactly what I've been afraid of all along. He doesn't even let his wife run the house! *He's* in the kitchen, and *he* serves, and *he* tells that beige savage what to do . . ."

Louise was about to remark that a husband "letting" his wife run the house was not necessarily a sign of his consideration for her, but before she could begin the "beige savage" himself strode in proudly, smiling, all trace of his former limp having disappeared. He cleared away a tray of coffee cups and strode out again.

"There," Mrs. Keeley whispered. "That's *exactly* what I mean about something odd going on here? Did you *see*?"

"See what?"

She pointed after Agador. *"He was barefoot."*

Chapter
forty-three

Albert couldn't seem to stop weeping; it had started from high emotion, but continued now from a low one. He was weighed down by shame.

Armand, Val, and Barbara were madly searching through the drawers and shelves of the powder room. Everywhere, masses of hair lay about, evidence of what the wig had once been. Val slipped on a shock of it and fell heavily on one knee. He yelped.

"Oh, I'm so sorry," said Albert, burying his face in his hands. "I've ruined *everything*!" He lowered his head and the wig slipped even further.

"Don't be silly," said Armand as he ransacked a drawer of cosmetics. "No one even noticed the wig. Where the hell is the spirit gum?"

"I don't know," Val said. "The girls carted everything out of here."

"I have a barrette," said Barbara brightly. She removed it from her hair and righted Albert's wig. "Let's try it. If you don't move your head too much, it might work . . ."

As she set about affixing it, Albert sniffed and said,

"Thank you. You're a very sweet girl. Oh, Val, I'm so sorry . . ."

"Do you hear something?" said Armand. They all stood quietly for a moment and listened.

They could hear, just barely, an occasional sharp word coming from the living room.

"We'd better hurry up and get back there," said Val.

The Keeleys were, in fact, trying to keep their voices down, but they were standing face-to-face now, fists balled with anger, snapping at each other; their self-control was slipping.

"I can't take much more of this 'poor Mrs. Coleman' business," said Louise. "I notice you didn't have this kind of blind sympathy for poor Bessie Jackson!"

"Bessie Jackson is an insensitive cow," the senator snarled. "This woman is a *lady.* For God's sake, I don't understand you! She's going to be *your* in-law, too."

"Well, if you think *he's* so terrible, maybe Barbara *shouldn't* marry his son!"

He shut his eyes in exasperation. "I don't think he's terrible in *that* way. I mean, he's not going to get mixed up in some stupid scandal. Europeans are like Republicans—they don't sleep with women who go on *A Current Affair.* Before Louise could jump in, he added, "Except for that moron Jackson."

She stared at him, feeling strangely dispassionate. "I don't think I've ever seen you before."

"What do you mean?"

"I don't know who you are. You aren't even worried about Barbara. Just your career. And 'poor little Mrs. Coleman.' "

"Oh, please." He all but stamped his foot in frustration. "You're just as worried about my career as I am. That's why you pushed for this marriage in the first place, remember? Yes, *you're* the one who pushed for it. And

the birdcage

Barbara can handle that boy. She's a modern woman—tough as nails. But Mrs. Coleman cries if you call her 'Mother.' She's that vulnerable. By God, it just breaks my heart! They don't make women like that anymore."

Louise took a step back from him. "I don't wa—"

She was interrupted by a knock on the door.

They stared at each other, not knowing what to do.

Another knock; then a breathless voice. "Hello? I'm home! I forgot my key."

Senator Keeley cleared his throat. "Who . . . who is it?"

"Oh, hello, it's Val's mother. Mrs. Goldman. Is Armand there?"

He looked at Louise. "Val's *mother*?" he whispered.

"Mrs. *Goldman*?" she whispered back.

"Hello?" the voice repeated, more insistently. "Armand, darling? Open up!"

"So *this* is the whole story," the senator hissed. "The son of a bitch has a live-in mistress!"

Louise, sensing a triumph for her point of view, started toward the door, calling out *"Coming!"*—just as Agador started for it from the opposite direction, calling out, *"Go away! You have the wrong house!"*

Louise reached the door first. She flung it open, and Katharine stepped in, looking poised and at-home, if a little winded.

Agador darted in front of Mrs. Keeley. "Good evening," he said to Katharine. "May I take your purse . . . as usual? Or . . . for the first time?" He was hopelessly confused; the story had got hopelessly mixed up somewhere.

Katharine didn't bother to correct him; she merely handed him her purse and said, elegantly, "Thank you." Then she turned to the Keeleys, who stood to one side, lips apart, brows knit. "You must be . . . Senator and Mrs.

Keeley?'' They nodded dumbly. She smiled at them and extended her hand; the Keeleys shook it limply. ''Katharine Goldman. I'm delighted to meet you. Please forgive me for being so terribly late, but I wa—''

''Sorry to take so long,'' came Albert's voice from around the corner. ''But Barbara wanted to see the rest of th—'' He rounded the corner and caught sight of Katharine, which almost caused the newly secured wig to flip right off his head. He stopped short, and Val, Barbara, and Armand bumped into him from behind.

He pointed at Katharine. ''What is *she* doing here?''

Armand scooted up to his side. ''Let me explain . . .''

''Yes,'' said the senator with the same righteous indignation that had won him three successive elections. ''Explain to all of us!'' He nodded toward Albert. ''I don't want to embarrass this lovely lady . . . but exactly how many mothers does your son have?''

''What?'' asked Armand.

He nodded his head in Katharine's direction. ''This woman has just introduced herself as Val's mother. *How many mothers does Val have?*''

It was all over now. But no one could write the epitaph except Val. Armand, Albert, Barbara, and Katharine all held their breath.

And Val . . . Val gave it a moment's thought and realized that there was nothing left. No trick, no stratagem, no sleight of hand remaining. Nothing at all . . . but the truth.

Gallantly, he walked up to Albert and gently removed the wig. Albert made a move to stop him, then gave up and allowed the revelation to occur.

''This,'' said Val, ''is my mother.''

Mrs. Keeley bit her knuckles and shrank back. The senator stared at Albert uncomprehendingly. And Albert?

Albert burst into tears and buried his face in Val's shoulder.

Val patted his back and continued addressing the Keeleys. "My father owns the nightclub downstairs. My mother is the star. Agador Spartacus's real name is Jake, and he's from New Jersey."

Agador gasped. "*No* one really needed to know *that*!"

Senator Keeley's eyes were dimming. "Wh-what . . ."

"We lied to you," said Val, disentangling himself from Albert, who had managed to regain some composure. He went and stood by Barbara; they clasped hands. "Your daughter and I . . . and everybody else lied for us. These are my parents." He gestured toward Armand and Albert.

Armand took Albert's hand. "And this is my wife." He turned to Katharine. "And this is the lady who gave birth to Val."

"Nice to meet you, Katharine," said Val.

"*Very* nice, Val," she said, a small lump in her throat. "You've done a good job, Armand."

Armand blushed. "Thank you." He put his hand on Albert's shoulder. "We're very proud of him."

Senator Keeley held up a finger. "I don't understand . . ."

"Wait a minute," said Louise, whose gears were busy turning. "That nightclub downstairs . . . he *owns* it?" She whirled on Barbara. "You mean, he's *not* a cultural attaché?"

"No," said Barbara, taking her cue from Val and tearing aside all the veils. "And he's not married to a housewife. And their name isn't Coleman. It's Goldman. They're Jewish."

The senator raised his finger higher. "I don't *understand*."

"He's a *man*," croaked Mrs. Keeley. "They're *both* men."

"He can't be." He looked at Albert. "You *can't* be Jewish."

"Kevin!" Louise barked, losing patience with him. "This is a *man*!"

He blinked. "What?"

"Don't you understand? They're *gay*. They own the drag club downstairs! They're *two men*!"

Albert summoned his courage and stepped forward. "I just want you to know, Senator Keeley," he said in a voice rinsed with emotion, "that I meant every word I said to you about a return to family values and a stricter moral code."

The senator nodded politely, then smiled and said, "I feel like I'm insane."

"Look, it's very simple," said Katharine, trying to be helpful. "Armand and I were together one night, an—"

"You *cried*," the senator said to Albert. "You said . . . you . . . I don't . . ."

"Kevin, nothing's changed," said Albert, trying to smile winningly. "It's still *me*. With one tiny difference."

The senator shook his head; he was beginning to feel faint. "I don't understand . . ."

"I'll explain it in the car," said Mrs. Keeley with iron in her voice. "Let's go. Barbara . . ."

Barbara gripped Val's hand and stood her ground. "No. I'm not coming."

Her mother shook her fist at her. "Oh, don't do this to me, Barbara. I may not be as 'vulnerable' as Mrs. Coleman— as whoever he is, but I still have feelings . . ." Suddenly, she broke down and started howling into her hands. "Oh . . . oh . . . *someone* has to like me best!"

They all stared at her, stunned. She sobbed uncontrollably, her knees shaking. Then Senator Keeley shook his head, as if waking from a dream, and put his arms around her shoulders.

"Take it easy," he said. "Take it easy, Louise." He looked around, looked at Albert, taking everything in as if for the first time. Then he looked away. "Barbara, we're leaving. And I want you to come with us."

"Daddy, *please* . . ."

"No, no arguing. I've made your mother cry, I'm coming up for reelection, we're in the middle of a scandal, and I'm in the home of a gay couple who own a drag club. Now, I understand that you want to get married, but how many lives do you want to ruin to do it?"

Her lower lip trembled. She looked at her father and her helplessly weeping mother. Then, feeling helpless herself, she turned to Val, Armand, and Albert.

"I would have . . . I would have really liked to have you as my family," she said haltingly, barely able to speak at all.

Then she quickly cut across the foyer to her father's side. He opened the door, then turned to Albert and said, "I just want to say, Mr. . . . Mrs. . . . Mr.—whatever your name is, that I hope this won't influence your vote."

"Senator Keeley!" brayed a voice from outside the door.

The senator turned in surprise and saw a camera staring him in the face. He ducked as the flash went off, then slammed the door.

He flattened his back against it and stretched his arms wide, as if forming a human barricade. A look of sheer animal terror gripped his face.

Chapter
forty-four

―――――

"id you get him? Did you get him?" asked Harry Radman.

Fishburn lowered his camera. "No," he said, frowning. "I would've, if you hadn't yelled out 'Senator Keeley.'"

Harry reddened in embarrassment. "I was just trying to make him turn."

They waited quietly; but they knew the door wasn't likely to open again. Harry pressed his ear against it and heard muted voices in excited conversation; eventually, the voices receded. He turned to Fishburn.

"We might as well head back downstairs," he said. "Stake out the corner of the street, so we can see this door *and* the front of the club. In case there's a way to get from one to the other."

They shuffled downstairs and headed back to the front of the building. Harry was relieved to see that the chauffeur and the limousine were still in place; the Keeleys weren't likely to have gone anywhere without their car and driver.

It was then that he noticed the WXLT van parked just

beyond, with a cameraman busily uploading equipment from the back.

He felt a burst of irritation; it stung his forehead. He turned to Fishburn and said, "Wait here." Then, making himself effectively invisible again, he approached the WXLT van to see what he could see.

He'd nearly reached it when a second van, this one bearing the call letters WLLS, drew up to the corner. A crewman jumped out of it and scooted over to the WXLT van, where, Harry now noticed, a young blond in an Alice in Chains T-shirt was lazily smoking by the passenger door.

The WLLS crewman tipped his baseball cap to the blond and said, "What's the story?"

She blew smoke in his face. "If you don't know, what are you doing here?"

"We got a call that *you* were here."

She took another drag, then exhaled. "My brother's a performer inside. Goes by the name of Helena Handbasket. I got our features editor to agree to a story on him, and the club. Love it if you gave him some extra publicity. Want me to get you a pass?"

The crewman squinted his eyes. "Hey, babe, I only *look* stupid."

She took another puff of her cigarette. "Yeah. Well. I won't argue there."

He turned in disgust and dashed back to his van, where he directed his people to start unloading their cameras.

Harry growled at the lot of them, then slipped back across the sidewalk to where Fishburn was keeping watch.

"What's the scoop?" asked the photographer.

Harry scowled and shook his head. "Those *vultures*," he spat, and he leaned against a newspaper box, settling in for what might be a very long wait.

Chapter
forty-five

Senator Keeley was stretched out on the chaise longue, his eyes staring wildly at nothing in particular, his breath coming hard and fast.

"Is he in shock?" asked Barbara, as she wept in Val's arms.

"Shocked, but not *in* shock," said Louise. She applied a cloth filled with ice to the side of his head. "He'll be all right."

Albert tapped her on the shoulder. "Open your hand," he said.

"What? I—" She faltered, then stuck out her hand and obeyed. He dropped two white tablets into her palm. "What are these?" she said, looking at them with no small horror.

"Pirin tablets," said Albert consolingly. "Make him take them."

"No, no," wailed the senator. *"Say no to drugs!"*

Louise frowned. "Well," she muttered, "if he doesn't want them . . ." She popped both into her own mouth and swallowed.

"I'm sorry, Kevin," said Albert. "I just thought-well, they do *wonders* for me!"

"The only thing that will do wonders for me is a quick, invisible exit." Suddenly he laughed desperately. "That's funny, isn't it? There's probably a mile-wide media circus around this godforsaken place by now."

Albert padded over to the window to take a look, passing Armand, who sat brooding in a chair, drinking from a bottle of bourbon, and Katharine, who was quietly eating a bowl of Guatemalan peasant soup.

Albert parted the curtains and peeked out onto the street. "Another television van just arrived," he said. "And a car. It says . . . *Florida Eagle*." He let the curtain fall, then turned happily and said, "Oh, that's just the print news!"

"They have a great headline," said the senator, trying to sit up. " 'Senator Jackson and his women—Senator Keeley and his men!' " Mrs. Keeley pushed him back down and applied the ice to the opposite side of his face.

"But it's perfectly innocent," she said. "You just came to meet the parents of the boy Barbara wants to marry. And you didn't know tha—"

"Louise, the people of this country aren't interested in details," he snapped. "They don't even *trust* details. They just trust headlines!"

"Well, if I can put in my two cents," said Katharine, as she gave her soup bowl to Agador for refilling, "they don't have a thing on you. It's their word against yours that you're even here."

"Well, they *will* have something on me," he said, mocking her optimistic tone, "because at some point I'll have to leave. People will *notice* if I'm never seen again." He turned to his wife. "More candy."

She frowned, then reached into her purse and gave him a chocolate mint.

Albert was peering through the curtains again. "Another TV crew," he said. "And they're going into the club. Wouldn't you know it? The one night I don't perform . . ."

"Well, Carmen should be fucking thrilled," mumbled Armand. He took another swig, then set the bottle aside; he was beginning to feel almost dangerously drunk.

Agador returned with Katharine's newly filled bowl, and handed it to her. "Can I get anyone else some soup?" he asked.

There was an instantaneous chorus of nos.

Katharine took another spoonful, then cocked her head and swallowed. "Who *made* this?"

Agador looked at her warily. "I did."

"Well, it's wonderful!" she enthused.

Barbara dried her eyes, then broke away from Val and went to crouch beside her father. "Daddy, I'm sorry . . ."

"I know," he said wearily, still sucking on the mint. "I know . . ."

"Another shot, senator?" Agador asked, proffering the bottle Armand had just abandoned.

He shook his head. "I don't really drink."

The houseboy smiled brightly. "Now is the time to pretend."

Armand got up and clicked on The Birdcage monitor so that he could hear what was happening in the club. Immediately, Cyril's voice filled the room. "—ank you for coming. And now we end as we began; our first number is our *last* number!"

The drumbeat grew in intensity, and then the Goldman Girls began wailing their signature tune.

"Pop," said Val, "couldn't the Keeleys slip out with the audience at the end of the show?"

202

"No," said Armand, shaking his head. "Those news-people are just *waiting* for that. They'd be recognized in two seconds."

Albert pursed his lips and gave Senator Keeley an appraising glance. "Not necessarily," he said, his voice dripping with implication.

Senator Keeley looked at him, bewildered.

"You're—you're *not,*" said Katharine, beginning to laugh hysterically. "Oh, no, Agador, I'm spilling your wonderful soup! Oh, I'm sorry, it's just so—" She looked at the senator and was suddenly possessed by laughter again.

"Is that woman deranged?" Senator Keeley asked, growing worried. "What on earth is she laughing at?"

"Oh," said Louise, now realizing what Albert was suggesting. "Oh, my! No, we couldn't possibly—we . . . we . . . Heavens, it *could* work, couldn't it?"

"Mm-hmm," said Albert, nodding.

She took her husband's jaw in her hand. "It'll take a lot of effort on your part," she said to Albert. "And we have so little time."

"Louise, for God's sake, stop pawing me like that," he said, growing *really* worried.

Albert put a finger on his chin and regarded the senator thoughtfully. "What season do you think he is?" he asked Mrs. Keeley. "I'm torn between autumn and summer."

She looked at him—looked at him like she'd never looked at him in all their years of marriage. Looked at him as if for the first time, as if seeking something new there. And, wondrously, finding it.

"Autumn," she said, nodding soberly. "Definitely autumn."

forty-six

═══════

he'd been plucked, slapped with makeup, and pushed into torturous and unrecognizable items of clothing. He'd been cooed over, cosseted, and infantilized by that degenerate Albert, who now mocked him by standing over him in a dark gray suit, combing out the wig he'd forced him to wear.

Now Albert stood behind him and placed his hands on the back of the chair. *"There!"* he said. "A hurried effort, of necessity, but on the whole a passable one. Now remember, the first time is always a big shock. Ready?"

And he spun him around to see himself in the mirror.

He stared. Something in the mirror bore a passable resemblance to himself. Something smeared with eye shadow and rouge and mascara and . . . and . . .

"Oh my God," he said with a sigh. His shoulders collapsed around his chest. His head dropped in defeat.

"Oh, now, come on," said Albert, slapping him on the back. "We can't *all* be Ingrid Bergman. You have many fine qualities . . . an inner . . . *strength.* And such authority! I think you look rather like the divine Marlene in *The Scarlet Empress.*"

"Oh my God," he said again.

Mrs. Keeley and Barbara entered, both in wild costumes of their own. Louise shrieked.

"Is that you, dear?" the senator asked pitifully.

She nodded hesitantly. "Yes," she said, her eyes boring holes into him. Finally, she said, "It's terrifying, Kevin."

"I know, I know." He got up, and moved behind the dresser. "Please turn away; I don't want you to see me like this."

"Oh, Kevin," she said, feeling for him.

He covered himself with a curtain. "I *told* them white would make me look fat."

There was a knock on the door. "Is everybody ready?" It was Armand.

"Not just ready—*radiant,*" called back Albert.

On his side of the door, Armand frowned; Albert *must* be exaggerating. He shrugged it off and said, "It's almost time. I'm heading downstairs now. Be on the alert!"

He flew down to the club, then raced to the microphone at the side of the stage just as the last strains of the finale were dying out. Armand grasped the mike and said, "A big hand for our girls, ladies and gentlemen!"

The music started up again, and the Goldman Girls trouped onto the stage, two by two, for their curtain call. Carmen was in her glory, taking a high kick with every step, flinging her arms high and glorying in the audience's cheers and wolf whistles. This was the night she'd been waiting for—her first chance to shine at center stage.

"As we come to the end of our show," said Armand into the mike, "*you* are family, too! Please sing along, now." He turned to the girls. "*One more time!*"

The applause erupted into a roar. Carmen, who had

only been too happy to agree to this prolongation of her own glory, began singing again, and gathered her "sisters" around her.

Scattered throughout the audience were newsmen, reporters, and a few photographers, their eyes darting around the darkened club, searching for their prey. Oscar and Faye were among them. Oscar was carrying a portable minicam on his shoulder, looking bulky and geeky and out of place: but Faye—Faye felt right at home. This is what nights in South Beach were made for—music and liquor and bodies and heat . . .

"Hey!" said Oscar, nudging her with his free elbow.

"What?" she said, annoyed. She was enjoying watching the ersatz girls parade around the stage to riotous applause.

"Who's that?" He pointed at a mustachioed, silver-haired man making his way through the crowd, grabbing hands like a politician.

"*Duh*, loser," she said in disdain. "It's the guy who was just talking into the microphone. Doesn't even *look* like Kevin Keeley." She gave him a slight sneer, then turned back to the stage and started swinging her rear end in time to the music.

Oscar, however, turned to watch Armand make his way through the crowd to the cash register behind the bar, where he leaned over and spoke to two strapping drag queens who were working the counter. A moment later, the two queens kissed him, then slipped through the crowd to the stage and disappeared behind the curtain.

Okay, wondered Oscar; what's going on here? And where is Kevin Keeley?

While Oscar's eyes were following the queens, Armand made his way to the front of the club, where he took a quick peek outside. Another truck had pulled up and was gorging forth media persons. The crowd of professionals on the premises was now pretty evenly divided between the inside of the club, and the outside.

Armand looked for Senator Keeley's chauffeur, whom Senator Keeley had said would be parked next to a streetlamp. Armand located him and was about to dodge out and inform the man of their plan; but then he spotted someone in a windbreaker peeling off bills and giving them to the chauffeur. And behind the man in the window waited a small line of others, each holding a wad of cash.

"So *that's* it," Armand muttered. The mystery of the Keeleys' discovery had been solved. He'd have to think of some other means of transporting them away—and think of it quickly.

He darted back inside, just as Harry Radman and Fishburn approached the front door. *"Jesus,"* said Harry. He tried to adopt his legendary aura of invisibility—but tonight, here at the entrance to The Birdcage, it failed him utterly, for the first time ever. He had to jostle, claw, and bulldoze his way through the door. By the time Fishburn caught up to him, he was winded and upset.

"How long do you think these guys will wait?" Fishburn asked, wiping his forehead with a Wendy's napkin.

Harry shook his head. "As long as it takes," he said unhappily. "There's no story if they don't get him coming out."

Coming out, thought Harry. Funny choice of words, there.

Chapter
forty-seven

When Kevin Keeley was four years old, his older sister Marigold had dressed him in some of her old clothes, stuck barrettes in his hair, and called him "Stephanie." They'd had a nice little tea party till their mother discovered them, punished Marigold, and told Kevin never to do that ever again.

When he was eighteen and being hazed by his fraternity, he and eleven other new pledges were made to put on angora sweaters, skirts, and nylon stockings and go to a campus mixer, where they had to offer themselves to the first upperclassmen they met. Kevin had escaped with a black eye that night . . . a black eye, and a lingering memory of the acute discomfort caused by nylons.

Now he was once again in women's clothing, and he couldn't help dreading that the outcome of this little gender-bending adventure was going to be even more unpleasant than either of those earlier disasters. Worse, this time he didn't even *look* good. Neither Shirley Temple—cute nor Amelia Earhart–athletic, he most closely resembled the kind of fat and ancient dowager whose hairy cheek he was always having to kiss at reelection time.

But he was resigned to his fate. Without this ruse, his career was over anyway. And if he were discovered sneaking out of this den of iniquity wearing Albert's taffeta nightmare, it would only mean that it was over with a substantially bigger bang.

It was almost time to go into action. Through the curtain, when he dared a peak, he could see the newsmen glancing impatiently at their watches, shifting their bulky cameras from shoulder to shoulder, while onstage Armand was waving his arms wildly, beckoning the show's drag queens—plus another two he'd recruited from behind the bar—to come onstage and join him as the terribly raucous musical number roared its way through its encore. There were excited cries from the crowd.

Senator Keeley suffered an attack of nerves: and it wasn't from fear of discovery. It was sheer performance anxiety.

"Yes, we're all family tonight," Armand enthused again into the microphone; then he turned to where Kevin stood in the wings, and waved him out.

Here goes, he thought, biting his lip. He tested his ankles for sturdiness, patted his tape-encased crotch, and hit the footlights.

The other drag queens waded off the stage and into the crowd, shimmying, shallying, bumping, grinding. Kevin followed suit; and from across the stage, he could see his wife and daughter—painted, padded, and plucked—doing the same.

He tried to make his way over to them. He was faintly aware that the way he was moving was profoundly out of rhythm with every other human being in the place, but if he just kept going, he might pass muster.

He stepped down into the crowd and started dancing through it toward the front door.

"Oh, great," said a lanky youth from beneath his camcorder as Kevin slipped by him. "I *hate* shows that do this."

Kevin sailed past him, snapping his fingers and smiling. If the poor kid only knew that the story of his career had just jangled right past him!

He kept moving, moving, taking care to shake his head every now and then to obscure his face with the ringlets of bright yellow hair. And of course, he had to remember to shuffle and bustle and swing his hips. It was degrading, but it worked.

And besides, degradation wasn't so bad. There was even an element of . . . a sort of . . .

No, no, there wasn't. Feeling that he'd just had a perilous moment on the brink of something unspeakable, he cast the thought aside and left it there to starve.

He passed a very annoyed-looking young woman in a T-shirt that said ALICE IN CHAINS. Whatever that meant. Probably some feminist conspiracy theory about how literary criticism has suppressed the children's heroine's innate lesbianism. He sniffed at the young woman, who caught him at it. She turned to her lanky, blank-faced coworker and said, "This show is really assaultive."

"I thought you were enjoying it," he said.

Kevin made sure to give her a bump as he passed. She glared at him and said, "Yeah. *Was* enjoying it. *Past* tense."

Her coworker laughed. "Know what you mean. Still . . ." He shrugged. "It's interesting."

Oh, brother, thought Kevin as he made his way nearer and nearer the door. The entire show, and the fellow dancers it had accrued, was just about to spill out into the street. Escape was almost within reach; he could see the streetlamps, actually see them!

A hefty, jowly, trench-coated man suddenly barred Kevin's way, looking for all the world like he'd lost a winning lottery ticket. His eyes darted everywhere, taking in everything in a kind of panic. A reporter, no doubt. Felt a good story slipping through his fingers. Kevin almost giggled, till he tried to squeeze past and the fellow turned and looked at him.

Right at him. Square at his face.

Kevin stopped himself before he could shriek: then he realized that shrieking was probably the best thing he could have done under these circumstances.

Instead, he tossed his head, sending his wig flying into his face, and pretended to sing. "And—and we da-dum thing . . . birds dee dee feather . . . la-la whatever . . ."

The reporter looked at him in disgust and moved hastily away.

Kevin's relief was immeasurable; but as he turned to make his final exit, he found that the party had stalled. The star drag queen—Carmen, was that her name?—had leapt atop a chair by the door and was commanding everyone to take partners and dance.

"What?" Kevin barked. "What's she . . ." He looked desperately around for Armand.

"Come on, everybody!" Carmen was shouting, clapping her hands above her head and gyrating madly. The engineers pumped up the music for a final flourish. *"Come on! Everyone grab a partner! Carmen sez you gotta!"*

Mere yards away, Louise Keeley froze. *Dance?* she thought. *Partner?* Who should she choose—a man or a woman?

While she was pondering this dilemma, an extremely handsome Latino took the decision out of her hands. He came up behind her and started grinding his hips into her backside, then whirled her around and began to tango as lustily as possible in such a dense crowd.

He dipped her, then pulled her back to his level, and just as she was feeling a measure of thrill at his mastery, he looked into her eyes and said, "I've never danced with another guy before."

Louise frowned. It would've been nice if she were just a *little* less convincing. She shrugged, lowered her voice, and growled. "There's always a first time."

They tangoed on.

Senator Keeley had managed to find his daughter in the crowd; she was the only other person still unpartnered.

He grabbed her hand, and when she turned and saw that it was him, she smiled and hugged him.

"No one will dance with me in this dress," he said to her, shouting over the music. "I *told* them white would make me look fat."

"I don't understand," said Barbara. "I'm as pretty as the rest of these guys."

Suddenly, Val appeared at her side. "Dance?" he said.

Both father and daughter piled into Val's open arms.

"Uh, wait," said Val, gently pushing the senator aside. "Not you, Barbara."

"Oh, come *on*, son," Kevin moaned, "don't leave me! I don't want to be the only girl not dancing!"

"Just keep moving toward the door," said Val, with an expression on his face that seemed to indicate he wasn't taking the senator's predicament entirely seriously. "We'll all be out of here in a minute. As soon as my pop can get Carmen to give up the spotlight."

He swept Barbara away, and Kevin turned to see that Armand was indeed ordering Carmen off the stool and out of the club. She was extremely reluctant to go, and was pretending, not very well, to be unable to hear him.

I'll never get out of here, thought Kevin in despair. He was a fat, middle-aged man, standing alone in a taffeta dress in the middle of a swirl of dancing couples. To be any more conspicuous, he'd need to burst into flame. He considered just giving himself up to the jowly, trench-coated hack, who was now inching closer again. Call it a day; let the media have their sacrificial lamb . . .

"Excuse me," said a suave, enchanting voice, rescuing him from the pit.

He turned.

Unbelievable.

It was Albert. Albert, in a tuxedo.

"Care to dance . . . baby?" Albert said with a wink.

Gratefully, Kevin stepped into his arms, and they fell into a waltz, while all around them the rest of the dancers created their own little worlds of dreams and delirium, until Carmen, now cajoled off her stool, led them out of the club and into the cool, clear, salt-laced air of the South Beach night. Traffic stopped, car horns blared, and the revelers dispersed in all directions, a dervish depleted of its energy, a community born in ecstasy now expiring in exhaustion.

Within moments, it was only a memory.

Chapter
forty-eight

Carmen was doubled over with sobs. "It'll never happen again!" she howled as Kiko and Beatrice led her over to the curb. She sat down, took off her heels, and bawled some more. "That asshole Armand! He used me to cover his sorry ass and then cut me off!"

Kiko and Beatrice plopped down on either side of her. "Well," said Beatrice, "it *was* the encore. And the idea *was* to get everyone out of the club so that the . . ."

"Who's side are you on?" Carmen snarled at her savagely.

Just across the street, Katharine sat at the wheel of her double-parked car, keeping the motor idling and the back door ajar, waiting for the Keeleys to dance their way into the street. They were still in some danger of discovery; some of the more alert newspeople had apparently caught on that the showgirl-led exodus might be a ruse, and were snaking about in front of the club, looking for anything suspicious. But Armand had said he'd provide a distraction . . . ah! That must be it now.

A man in a business suit, with a copy of the *Washington Post* in front of his face, appeared at the side of the building and started walking down the street in the opposite direction from the club. Immediately, the journalists stampeded after him. And Harry Radman, despite his bulk, was at the head.

Oh, God, thought Harry as he raced toward his prey: *oh, God, please let it be him. I couldn't have been this stupid . . .*

And then he was on him, and before the microphones could dive at the man's face, Harry had spun him around and pulled the newspaper away.

"Shit," he said, abandoning all hope. "This isn't him. This guy's Spanish."

"Hispanic," said Agador, correcting him. "And in fact I'm Guatemalan."

As he ambled away, Fishburn caught up with Harry. "Man," he said, "I coulda *told* you not to go after him. Didn't ya see?" He pointed down. "Guy's *barefoot.*"

"*Damn* it," said Oscar to Faye. "That was really stupid. Now we *know* he was in there."

They all looked around in defeat, not knowing what to do next.

By this time Katharine had caught sight of the *real* senator; no mistaking that wig, in however much disarray. She put the car into gear and moved into traffic slowly, while the driver behind leaned on his horn in disapproval.

She pulled up alongside the Keeleys and kept pace with them. They appeared not to notice her. She tapped her horn, but in the general chaos, her honk was drowned out by a dozen others—and Carmen's angry bawling smothered them all.

"I don't believe it," Mrs. Keeley was telling her family. She held up a fistful of twenty-dollar bills and said, proudly, "I made a hundred dollars!"

The senator ignored this and pulled his wife and daughter toward their limousine. "Remember, keep dancing," he ordered them. "We're not out of the woods yet."

"But this isn't the *plan*," wailed Barbara in protest, trying to drag her heels.

"It is now," he said. "I'm not saying I'm not grateful to Armand, but the sooner I'm in control of my own destiny again, the better."

"Over here!" Katharine called out. *"Yoo-hoo!"*

Kevin turned at her and executed a little wave. "All right," he said, "you two go and join her. I've got to go and talk to the chauffeur. I'm only going to have Katharine take us a couple of blocks, to El Dorado and Palm: then, we'll get back in our own car and be captains of our destiny again." And he danced away, his steps now taking on a spastic, dervishlike air.

Louise and Barbara looked at each other worriedly, then dashed across the street and leapt into Katharine's car.

The senator sidled up to the limousine's driver door, shaking his hips and shoulders. From inside, the chauffeur looked at him in horror, then cringed.

Kevin bent over, stuck his head through the window, and winked to signal his real identity. "Meet me in twenty minutes on the corner of El Dorado and Palm," he said in a low voice.

The chauffeur started the engine and put the car into gear. "Lady, not for a million dollars!" he said, rolling up the electric window.

Kevin barely pulled his neck free in time, and was just about to consider whether he might pound his fists through the glass and strangle his employee, when he heard his wife and daughter's voices calling. *"Over here! Come on!"*

He turned and saw them safely tucked into Katharine's car.

Sighing in resignation, he did a limpid mambo across the street and joined them.

epilogue

---

the bells pealed; the organ played; the congregation stirred with excitement and emotion.

And the wedding began.

And if it truly is a faux pas of the first rank to outshine the bride, how then to forgive the left side of the church? For forgiveness was indeed in order. None of those seated on the right side of the church knew the details—or even the rough outline of the events that had transpired in South Beach—but when Senator Kevin Keeley (R.-Ohio) and his wife, Louise Madden of Cincinnati, made it clear that there was to be no ostracism of any kind of the . . . well, the *persons* connected to the groom . . . in whatever way—well, the speculation among their guests was, in a word, heated.

And as Barbara Keeley made her way up the aisle on the arm of her father, who appeared genuinely happy in spite of everything—well, sure enough, every pair of eyes on the *right* side of the church was fixed not on the bride's gown, which her mother had worn before in her 1967 and her grandmother before that, in 1944, but on the *left* side of the church, where the groom's family sat amidst a buzzling knot of . . . well, *theatrical* persons was the only term most of the guests could manage, and that was pushing euphemism to the limit of its usefulness. Because while one had had to grow accustomed to theatrical persons in the past twenty years, such condescension had usually to rise above nothing more objectionable than conspicuous consumption, or exceptionally vocal Marxism, or extraordinary fertility outside of marriage. What one had in *no* way grown accustomed to was gentlemen of the theatrical profession sporting cinched waists and crinoline and hats with veils, uttering in stage whispers such unutterables as "Robert Dole is *gorgeous.*"

None of which measured as anything against the distress of the matron of honor, one Bitsy Rowe-Hanley of Atlanta, who stood stock-still during the ceremony, her lavender gown's elbow-length sleeves concealing her trembling shoulders as she regarded her partner in the processional, the best man, a Guatemalan (if the gossip was correct) who had even for this august occasion, eschewed shoes.

Even the celebrants themselves were cause for discomfort, for in addition to a perfectly respectable minister from the Keeleys' hometown, there was a rabbi (invited by the groom's father) who not only looked like Bette Midler, but gave every impression that he had actively *endeavored* to look like Bette Midler. His smile was not so much beatific as anticipatory, as though at any moment he might grab a microphone and start crooning the theme song from *Beaches.*

And what was there to say, really, about the groom's father's . . . *friend*? Who, in his mauve tuxedo, had been guided to his place in the pew just before the processional began, as though he were in fact the groom's mother? And who wept and keened during the ceremony into what even those across the aisle could tell was a heavily scented handkerchief? What was there to say, indeed, that could be said within the confines of a family gathering held by an esteemed colleague, a senator of impeccable credentials, a man of traditional values, a family man, a Christian, a man of moral fiber and indomitable righteousness—a man who had braved with stoic silence the storms of public opinion for the sake of his daughter, even to the point of allowing the media to congregate like wolves outside this very church?

There was only one thing to be said. And it was said, over and over, by each and every one of them, as they greeted Albert later in the receiving line, where he stood between Armand and Senator Keeley, shaking hands and holding back his tears:

"Such a pleasure to meet you. Lovely wedding. You must be so proud."